Gracie & Zeus Live the Dream

ELIZABETH RODERICK

1

Grace Morgan was fast asleep, dreaming her ex-husband's testicles were caught in his bicycle chain.

He stood on the corner of a busy intersection, tugging at his anatomy with a consternated expression, but they wouldn't budge. Eventually, he gave up and trudged down the damp sidewalk, his spandex shorts wrapped around his ankles, his nut sack stretching out like silly putty as he dragged his bicycle behind him.

A cell phone's buzzing jangled the pleasant tableau, and it slipped away. Grace sighed, rolled over, and peeled her eyelids open.

"Ohmygod!" She flinched from the staring, golden-hazel eyes of her adult foster son, Zeus.

"It's your phone, Gracie," Zeus said. His face was scant inches from hers as her phone continued to buzz against her pressboard nightstand.

Grace struggled to get air into her uncooperative lungs. "What the hell are you doing, Zeus?"

He gazed at her unblinkingly. "It's your phone."

Grace sat up, blinking blearily at the walls of the please-don't-tell motel.

"Don't answer it," Zeus said. "They just want to talk about the Mayan Calendar, but it's a hoax. It's not always May."

Grace shoved Zeus out of the way and pawed through the cups of congealed noodles and shreds of candy wrappers on the nightstand. Zeus scooted over to stay in her line of sight, his gaze unwavering, his pupils gigantic. "I'm all out of Adderall, Gracie."

Grace cursed. "Seriously? It was supposed to last until Monday."

"Maybe you should ask that Mayan on the phone if they have more."

She finally found her phone and cursed again when she saw the number on the screen. Lawrence Shaupin, the commissioning editor for *High Note Magazine*. She hit the answer button. "Hello?"

Zeus crawled forward to peer at the bedside lamp. "I think that light bulbs have their own kind of consciousness."

With a seething glare at her foster son, Grace sprang from bed. "I'm sorry, say that one more time, Lawrence. I think we have a bad connection." She sidestepped the tower of mini-shampoos Zeus had built at the bottom of his bed and dodged into the bathroom, locking the door behind her.

"I said, good morning, Grace," Lawrence repeated.

Grace attempted to pull herself together. *Remember who you're talking to. Remember your career.* Maybe injecting some sex appeal into her voice would help. "Hey. How are you?"

There was a short silence on the other end. "You okay? You sound sick."

Grace pinched the bridge of her nose and cleared her throat. "No, I'm fine. What's up?"

"I got a story for you."

Grace's heartbeat quickened. "Oh?"

"Inez Carter is in town, and word has it she's involved with Nicole Watters, better known as BeatBot."

"BeatBot. Isn't that the dubstep girl who wears the freaky pants?"

"That's the one."

Grace leaned on the cluttered laminate countertop, her veins flooding with adrenaline. Inez Carter, the lead singer for Karma Korn, was quickly becoming a car accident the world couldn't look away from. Even a superficial article about her could get international exposure. "Sounds hot. Did Inez dump her girlfriend, then? Jacob Easley's daughter?"

"That's what we need you to find out."

Grace rolled her eyes at her reflection in the mirror. Of course the story was superficial. But hopefully the public's insatiable appetite for bullshit would earn her enough for a deposit on an apartment. "What's the lead?"

"I'll give you the details. You ready?"

"Just a sec." She poked through the flotsam on the bathroom counter until she found an eyeliner pencil. "Let me find some paper." She searched under the bath toys Zeus had constructed out of used toothpaste tubes and twisted wire hangers, but there was nothing to write on. She was about to scrawl it on the mirror when Zeus began vocalizing the guitar solo for *Stairway to Heaven* right outside. His long fingers pushed a folded scrap of notebook paper under the door. Grace snatched it and unfolded it.

From now on, my name is 697.34, it said. *Also, I want a mandolin.*

Grace spread the paper on the counter. "Go ahead." She scrawled down the information Lawrence gave her, promised to meet him soon for drinks, and hung up.

She sighed, leaned against the cigarette-burnt Formica countertop and studied the dark circles under her brown eyes. Lawrence was an old friend from college, and her one and only contact in the industry. It was wrong to lead him on, but she really needed the work.

Zeus stopped singing. "What are you doing in there? Is it something cool?"

"Taking a shower." Grace squinted to check the progress of her crow's feet.

"Don't use my soap."

Grace didn't want to look at the huge mound of squished-together motel soap he'd amassed on a corner of the tub, but she couldn't stop herself. "Don't worry."

She tore herself from the mirror and reached around the yellowed plastic shower curtain to turn on the water. A noise like hail on a car roof assaulted her ears, and she quickly turned it off again.

Peering cautiously into the tub, she grimaced.

"Oh, I forgot about my fort," Zeus said. He wiggled his fingers under the door. "Don't mess with it. There's pizza in there, but it's under the tarp, so it should be okay."

Grace pressed her fingertips into her throbbing eyelids.

2

Zeus scrabbled around on the floorboards of the car, tossing aside empty iced tea bottles and crumpled napkins. Grace tried to keep her eyes on the road, wishing she'd ignored his tantrum and left him back at the motel. "Zeus, do you have to do this now?"

"Just a minute. I know I left one of my brain toys down here somewhere." He burrowed deeper under the dashboard, and his foot kicked out, catching her shoulder.

Grace's hand jerked on the wheel, and the car swerved over the yellow line, directly into the path of a truck hauling a load of port-a-potties. She yanked the wheel, her life flashing before her eyes as the honking truck barely missed her. Being flattened by a shit-mobile would have been a consistent end to it. "Dammit, Zeus!" she barked as she straightened the wheel. "Sit in your seat like a big boy."

"Coming," he said sheepishly. His butt wiggled in the air as he tried to twist around, then went still. "Gracie. I think I'm stuck, Gracie."

She risked a glance. He'd somehow gotten one of his legs all the way under the passenger seat. "Zeus-"

He twitched and writhed, and the underside of the dash made a horrible cracking noise. "I'm super, super serial, Gracie. Help me, Gracie."

She clutched a hand in her hair, which ruined twenty-five minutes of styling work. She tried to smooth the short, golden curls back into place. "Godammit! I'm gonna be late."

"But I'm trapped! Help! This isn't a cool situation!"

She sighed and pulled off into the parking lot of a strip mall.

As she got out and tried to tug him free, she asked herself, as she did fifty times a day, how her life had come to this.

Five years previously, Grace Morgan and her then-husband Mitch had decided to take in foster children. It was Mitch's idea; he said he wanted to further the cause of socioeconomic equality, to "give back to the community that has blessed us with so much prosperity."

Grace suspected he just wanted something to be self-righteous about at parties.

Before their first placement, the social worker called them in for a conference.

"The boy's mom got busted for cooking meth," the woman said. "Her son, Zeus, is fifteen and he's…well, he's troubled. But with a stable environment, we hope he'll flourish."

He certainly flourished, like an uncontrolled outbreak of plague. Zeus spent the first week growling at Mitch every time he walked into the room and refusing to eat anything but canned tuna. When he started sleeping curled up at her feet, Grace wanted to ship him back to the agency.

Mitch refused. "You can't just give up on a person. How would you feel if someone gave up on you just because you were having a hard time?"

Grace agreed to give Zeus a few more weeks. A few days later, he'd rummaged in a closet and found one of Grace's guitars.

Zeus loved the instrument more than he loved canned tuna and was soon playing it like Hendrix, if Hendrix had taken a good deal more drugs. When Zeus wrote an epic ballad about a pigeon falling in love with Woody Allen, and sang it using actual words in the English language, Grace decided he could stay.

Three years after that, Mitch had left Grace for a top-heavy yoga instructor. When Zeus turned eighteen a few weeks later, Grace hadn't had the heart to kick him out into a world he was ill-equipped to deal with alone.

Most of the money had left when Mitch had, so Grace had taken Zeus to the Social Security office to apply for assistance, with Zeus as Exhibit A. During the meeting, he'd wrestled Grace's socks off her feet and performed an X-rated puppet show starring Woody Allen and an amorous pigeon. At the end of the meeting, the benefits examiner gave Grace a tearful hug and the government checks kept coming in.

Grace wrapped her arms around Zeus's still-stuck torso and tugged in consternation. "Come on, Zeus. Help me out."

He flailed, and his head cracked against the bottom of the glove box. "Ow! I think I just made myself more mentally disabled."

"I doubt it," Grace muttered. Finally, after a short struggle, his leg came free, and they both tumbled to the pavement in a tangle of limbs. Grace's head landed with a wet crunch on a discarded paper cup. The remnants of the drink infiltrated her carefully coiffed hair.

She lay there, watching pigeons flap across the hazy blue sky.

Zeus gently patted her all over. "Are you hurt, Gracie? I think I made you skin your butt."

"I'm fine."

He took her hand. "Do you need me to call an ambulance?"

"No, I'm okay." She pried herself from his grasp and stood up.

He got up, too, and dusted her suit off for her. "You still look proper."

Grace patted her hair, cringing when she felt a sticky mass of glued-together ringlets. "I don't know about *proper*."

"Ooh, you have grape slushy in your hair." He stepped closer and licked it. "Mmm, you taste like a lollipop. I wonder how many licks it'd take to get to the Tootsie Roll inside."

She pushed him away as he came at her again with his tongue outstretched. "Come on, Zuzu. Maybe we can still make it on time."

Zeus slowly drew his tongue back into his mouth. He nodded, his head hanging. His too-long brown curls covered his face, and he strongly resembled a reprimanded springer spaniel. They climbed into the car.

Zeus picked at a scab on his knee as they pulled out of the parking lot, his lips pursed into a frown. Grace glanced his way and sighed inwardly, then pulled down the visor and checked her reflection.

"Shit," she muttered, pulling apart the sticky tangles with her fingers. "Doesn't look too bad, right? Maybe they'll think I just went heavy on the product."

"Sometimes I feel like people would be better off without me," Zeus said.

Grace winced and flipped the visor closed. "Zeus, can we not do this right now?"

He shot her an injured look from the corner of his golden eyes. "If someone doesn't care about someone else, they shouldn't pretend they do. It just makes for hurt feelings when the real emotional situation becomes apparent."

"Zeus-"

He blew a raspberry.

She huffed. "Would you please—" He cut her off with another raspberry, but she spoke over it. "If *I don't start earning some money soon, we're going to starve.* Do you understand? No more pizza or action figures. I need to get to this interview!"

Zeus bounced up and down in his seat, exploding with raspberries during the whole speech.

Grace gave up, gripping the steering wheel and staring out the windshield in silence. Her future spread out in front of her, as bleak as the smoggy horizon. She'd fail as a freelancer in L.A. and end up back home with her parents, picking up temp work as an office drone. Zeus would end up as just another cart-wheeling bum, or in an institution.

She could feel his eyes on her. Then he pressed his forehead into his knees, quietly singing *Paint it Black*.

Fifteen minutes of morose singing later, they pulled up to the address Lawrence had provided. She spent another ten minutes driving around looking for parking before she finally pulled into the employee lot of a machine parts factory. She chose a spot that looked inconspicuous, shut off the engine, and checked her watch. "Only twenty minutes late. Now listen, Zeus—"

"Now listen, Zeus."

She gritted her teeth. "I need you to stay here and watch the car—"

"I need you to stay here and watch the car."

She smacked him on the shoulder, and he glanced over at her with a slight grin before facing forward with a look of deliberate innocence.

"I shouldn't take too long. If the parking attendant comes, just…just talk to him, okay? Maybe they'll let us off as a charity case."

Zeus picked at his knee again, his grin fading. He nodded.

"Thanks." She got out and headed for the studio entrance.

A beefy guy in mirrored aviators stood sentry outside the door, three people lined up in front of him.

"I write for a very popular music blog, *The Night of the Living Dude*," the one in front pleaded. "We get almost a thousand hits a day. It would be great publicity for the band."

"That's what Karma Korn needs, is more publicity," the security guy drawled. He raised his chin slightly, and Grace could feel him watching her from behind his sunglasses. "And who are you?" he asked. "You write for *Suzie's Super Opinions on Music* blog or something?"

The others turned to watch her suspiciously. Grace swallowed, giving the goon her best smile. "I'm Grace Morgan. Lawrence Shaupin from *High Note* sent me to do an article about Karma Korn's new album."

The goon's eyebrows inched slightly higher as the three other hopefuls shuffled their feet. Flies buzzed around the sticky spot in Grace's hair. "*High Note*," the goon said. He gazed off toward the potted palms flanking the entry, clicking his tongue against the roof of his mouth. "There's already a chick in there says she's doing an article for High Note. *Nice chick.* Looks like that actress in all the action movies, except lankier, more freckles."

Grace's heart sank. *Marla Pocchino.* "I know her, she's another freelancer."

The three supplicants smirked. In her head, Grace cursed Lawrence for pitting her against another journalist. She wondered if Marla had to lead him on with promises of dates, too, or if she'd gotten the assignment based on talent alone. Marla was at least seven years younger than Grace, but she already had two published novels. Grace hadn't read them. She was afraid they'd actually be good.

Grace had been struggling to finish a novel for almost eight years.

The security guy watched Grace with crossed arms. Sweat soaked into the cheap fabric of her pantsuit as she waved the flies from her hair. Finally, the guy nodded. "Go ahead."

"Thank you." Grace smiled. The other reporters glared daggers at her as she sidestepped them. "Excuse me," she muttered sweetly.

She passed through the smoked glass door into a reception area. The hardwood walls were lined with gold and platinum records. A young woman behind a desk glanced up from her cellphone, flinging her asymmetrical bangs from her eyes to squint at Grace. "Another journalist or something? Go on in. I think they're editing vocal tracks in the studio, but some people are hanging out in the lounge."

"Okay, thanks." Hopefully, all wasn't lost.

Grace went through another door into a hallway. The sound of voices came from a room near the end, and she headed toward it, straightening her jacket and patting her hair. One last sugar-drunk fly fell to the floor tiles, buzzing with contentment.

She entered and found several people sprawled on couches with beers and plates of food in their laps. Grace thought she recognized Karma Korn's drummer loading up at the buffet, his beard like a rust-red dish scrubber on his chin. The only other person she knew was the young woman leaning on the wall beside a potted palm, gesturing carelessly with a buffalo wing as she spoke.

"So when the cops showed up, we were like, 'No way, who would want to steal George Clooney's iguana?'"

The crowd erupted in laughter. The woman paused with the chicken wing halfway to her mouth as her eyes fell on Grace. She smiled lazily as the laughter died away. "Hey, Grace."

"Hey, Marla."

A look of benign interest flickered in the other reporter's large, green eyes. She had creamy, freckled skin. A cascade of wavy, strawberry-blonde hair fell below her perfectly poised shoulders.

Grace wiped a bead of sweat from her nose, feeling sticky and old.

"Everyone," Marla said, "this is Grace Morgan. She's a freelance journalist, too. She used to be a reporter for a paper in Seattle, back when newspapers existed." Marla smiled. Grace smiled back, which set a muscle in her eye twitching.

"Seattle, huh?" one of the guys on the couch said. He crossed his legs, which looked like burnt matchsticks in his tight, black jeans. "Good music scene up there, right?"

"Uh, yeah," Grace said. "In fact, I used to play in a couple bands."

"Oh really?" the guy said. "What bands?"

"One was called Selling the Sofa. The other was a Journey cover band called Streetlights People."

At the buffet, the drummer laughed. "Journey. That's awesome."

She smiled at him, realizing she didn't even know his name. She'd meant to research Karma Korn a bit before she'd come, but had been distracted by Zeus's theory that if she left him behind in the motel room the maid would vacuum him up and sell him to the Knights Templar.

"I didn't know you played, Grace," Marla said. "Selling the Sofa. Have I heard of them? Did you guys play South by Southwest?"

Grace clutched her elbows. "Yeah, but that was after I left the band."

"Ah," Marla said delicately. Her smirk made Grace want to projectile vomit all over her face.

"I remember you," the drummer said. "Selling the Sofa's a great band, but I think you're much better than the guy they replaced you with." He gestured at the buffet. His beard twitched, and Grace thought he might be smiling. "Have some eats."

"Thanks." He probably didn't really remember her—the band hadn't had much exposure when she was in it—but she was eternally grateful to him for the look Marla was giving her now.

As Grace looked over the food, her stomach growled loudly, reverberating through the quiet room. Several people laughed, including the drummer. "Your belly monster likes the idea of food."

Grace picked up a plate, trying to hide her embarrassment. "Freelancing is hungry work."

The truth was, she hadn't eaten since breakfast the day before. Zeus cost as much to feed as a herd of circus elephants, and their budget was tighter than guy-on-the-couch's pants.

The drummer's eyes crinkled slightly as he held out a hand to her, and Grace realized he was actually sort of cute, for a tangled pile of hair. "I'm Nelson, by the way," he said.

"Yeah, I know," she lied. "You're the drummer, right?"

"Yes. I hit things with sticks for a living."

Grace laughed, her cheeks heating. His hand was warm, and calloused from his drumsticks. It felt nice in hers. She hoped he wouldn't notice she had slushie in her hair.

A sharp voice punctured the magical moment like a poisoned needle. "Oh, my God, who are all these *people*?"

Nelson let go, and Grace turned to see a young woman with long, cherry-red hair flounce through the doorway, a scowl on her heavily-made-up face.

The infamous Inez Carter.

She was followed by two ambling young men and a short girl whose burgundy lips were tiny and round, like a sphincter. They were Karma Korn's bassist, guitarist, and keyboard player, if Grace remembered correctly.

Inez's eyes narrowed when her gaze fell on Grace, and she wiped her nose along the entire length of her skinny arm before turning to glower at Nelson. "Did you let the *media* in here, Nelson?"

Grace shifted on her feet, exchanging a nervous look with Marla.

"What am I, security?" Nelson said. "Besides, you expected to not have the media here? Are we suddenly shunning the spotlight?"

"What am I, security?" Inez repeated mockingly, then waggled her pierced tongue at him, her nose scrunching to half its normal length. She huffed like a badly calibrated steam engine. "I don't want any fucking reporters or hangers-on in here. I can't deal with this today. I'm on my period, and I need a bowl of meatball pho before I kill someone."

Grace's shoulders slumped. Would she even get another opportunity at a high-profile story like this? She'd been lucky to get this one.

Then Nelson caught Grace's eye with a helpless and apologetic look, and her heart beat a little faster. Maybe there was still a chance, if she could get his number…

A commotion in the hallway brought the scene within the room to a standstill. A man's voice yelled "Hey! You can't go in there!"

Zeus called back, "Don't shoot! We're both members of the same galactic army!"

Grace let out an anguished moan, the remainder of her hope evaporating as Zeus tumbled through the door, almost knocking over Inez and the rest of her band. He was followed closely by the furious-looking security guard.

"He busted in," the guard said. "I tried-"

"Don't listen to a word he says," Zeus said. "I think he took the wrong pills and it scrambled his programming." He grinned at Grace, who was frantically calculating how much food she could grab from the buffet before they were tossed out.

Then Zeus's eyes found Inez. His smile went lopsided as he smoothed the curls back from his face. "Hey." His voice was subtly deeper. "Do you like guys who can throw lightning bolts?"

Inez blinked. She was still sneering but looked like she was having a hard time maintaining it.

Zeus held up the paper bag he was carrying. "Do you want some dim sum? I talked to the lady in the restaurant, and she was happy to give us provisions for the cause, as long as I made Godspeed. And every speed is Godspeed for me, because I'm Zeus."

The security guard grabbed Zeus's arm, but Zeus didn't seem to notice. He was too busy staring at Inez, who thrust her tattooed cleavage toward him and smiled with crimson lips.

"Come on, you crazy shit," the guard said, yanking Zeus toward the doorway, but Inez held up a hand.

"No, wait." Her hungry gaze slid from Zeus's face to the bag of food. "Do you have pork buns in there?"

"I have tons of buns," Zeus said, his eyes widening suggestively. "Tons and tons of buns."

"I like buns," Inez said, jiggling a little.

Grace raised an eyebrow. She must be misreading the signs. Inez Carter was the current poster child for flamingly, openly gay.

Inez shot the security guard a withering look. "Jason, let him go. Get back to guarding, or whatever. He's all right."

Grace couldn't see the goon's eyes behind his sunglasses, but she figured he must be sizing Zeus up against Inez's assertion that he was "all right" and finding it doubtful. But he shrugged and let go of Zeus's arm. "Okay. Whatever."

He started to leave, but Inez stopped him. "Hold on." She glared at Grace. "I want you to take the reporters out of here. And that guy, too, whoever he is." She pointed a blue fingernail at the guy in the tight, black pants.

"Hey, I'm the trumpet player you hired."

"Okay, not him, but these two chicks are totally reporters. I can smell it on them." She sniffed the air. "Blech."

Grace and Marla exchanged another look, their disappointment creating a tenuous solidarity between them. Grace began loading cheese and grapes onto her plate as fast as she could. The guard started toward her, but Zeus stepped in front of him.

"No way," Zeus said. "Gracie is my bestest friend. If she goes, my buns and I are marching right, straight out of this freak show with her." He hugged the paper bag of food defiantly and raised his eyebrows at Inez.

The singer twisted a lock of hair around her finger, glancing between Zeus and Grace. Grace stood paralyzed, barely able to hope. After a moment, Inez shrugged. "Okay, fine. Goldilocks can stay. But the other reporter chick goes."

Marla opened her mouth, then closed it again, her already pale face going completely bloodless. The guard looked unhappy, but he laid a gentle hand on her shoulder. "Okay, come on. You heard Queen Eenie." As he escorted Marla out, Grace couldn't keep the triumphant grin from her face, or stop herself from twiddling her fingers in farewell.

Zeus caught Grace's eye and shot her a quick thumbs-up, as if this had been his plan all along.

3

Grace found herself in the control room with the members of Karma Korn while the hired horn players laid down their tracks. The unexpected source of her luck currently sat huddled with Inez on a loveseat, feeding her pieces of dumpling. Zeus was helping a potsticker pirate fight off an egg-tart soldier during a retreat to the seaside-cave sanctuary of Inez's mouth.

Inez giggled and smacked Zeus's cheeks with a slice of barbecued pork. She seemed to think Zeus's behavior was normal enough, and Grace wondered if perhaps the singer spent too much time in the company of other musicians.

Nelson sat next to Grace on another loveseat, stroking his beard as he watched Inez and Zeus. "Your friend certainly has a vivid imagination."

Grace shifted uncomfortably. "Yeah, well, he may be a bit… weird… but he had a rough childhood. I took him in as a foster kid, originally." She squared her shoulders. "He's actually super cool once you get to know him."

"No, no, he *is* super cool. Weird, but cool." Nelson smiled. "That's really nice of you, to take him in like that."

Grace shrugged. "He sticks by me, even though I'm a little weird, too, so I return the favor." She thought back to the time right after Mitch had left when Zeus had talked her out of joining the Marines or the Hare Krishnas. He'd made her eat and coaxed her to leave the house when she otherwise might have never gotten out of bed again.

Nelson was giving her a worried look, so she pulled herself back to the present and made herself smile. "Anyway, I guess I wouldn't be here with you if it weren't for him, so I should be even more thankful I have him as a friend."

"I would've figured out a way to keep you from getting booted, even if he hadn't stepped in, but yeah."

Grace's cheeks warmed. *You're here for the story, that's all,* she told herself. *You promised yourself you wouldn't date. Never. Ever. Never again.*

She sat up straighter and grinned in what she hoped was a sheepishly disarming way. "So. Uh. Is it true Inez broke up with Mildred Easley? Is she seeing Nicole Watters, aka BeatBot now?"

Nelson's eyes narrowed, and he laughed. "Oh, yeah, I almost forgot. You're writing an article."

She shrugged, ducking her head. "I've gotta make a living somehow."

He looked over at Inez, his expression guarded. "Yeah, it's true. She dumped poor Mil to take up with Nicole."

Grace had a small moment of relief—she had at least the beginnings of her story—but the relief was tempered by guilt for turning a completely normal conversation into a fishing expedition.

But she was a *reporter* for fuck's sake. Real reporters wouldn't feel guilty for chasing a story.

Nelson leaned back and stretched his legs out. "So. You play keyboard, right? You play any other instruments?"

"I also play the guitar and saxophone," she replied, glad to change the subject.

He grinned. "Saxophone. Awesome. You playing in any bands now?"

"Not since I quit Selling the Sofa five years ago."

He examined her, combing his fingers through his beard. "Why did you quit that band, anyway? I've heard them, they're good. Were there just too many, you know, artistic differences?"

Grace fought back her desire to feign diarrhea and end the conversation. "Naw. I just needed to concentrate on my editorial job."

He cocked a teasing eyebrow. "What tips can you give me, as a journalist, for making an interviewee less evasive?"

She snorted, twisting her fingers together. Was she that easy to read? Nelson's eyebrow cocked higher; she hesitated, but something about him inspired confidence.

"My ex-husband convinced me to quit playing. He said I needed to grow up. Then he left me for a 22-year-old."

Nelson broke into a slow grin, then laughed. It was so infectious and goofy that she found herself joining in. It was the first time she'd laughed about her divorce.

"What an ass," he said. "You should start playing again. We should jam sometime."

Grace's traitorous heart sped up. "I'd like that."

Inez's giggle drew Grace's eye. Zeus was braiding chow mein noodles into the singer's hair.

One of the engineers shot them a stern look. "I don't mean to be Captain Killjoy, but we're trying to work here. It's hard to hear the tracks with you making all that noise."

Zeus stopped braiding and adopted a deadly sober expression. Grace had a sick moment of dread, sensing what was about to happen. "Zeus-"

Too late. He threw a noodle at the engineer's face, where it stuck firmly, held by a generous coating of sauce.

Grace squeezed her eyes shut against tears of frustration and anger. Inez fell back on the sofa, convulsed with laughter. The engineer stood and pointed a shaking finger at Zeus. "You. Out. Now."

Inez stifled her giggles, and there was a ringing silence in the control room. Zeus's face crumpled as he realized what he'd done.

Inez scowled at the engineer. "Get over yourself. You can't take a stupid noodle to the face? I want him here. He's hilarious."

The engineer opened a cabinet and pulled out a napkin. "It's time you sent your playmates away and got some work done."

Inez opened her mouth to retort, but Karma Korn's manager, a man who looked like he had a bad style consultant telling him how to look young and hip, stood and whispered something in her ear. His assistant, a younger and somewhat awkward man, made a move toward Zeus.

Grace rose quickly and grabbed Zeus's arm before the assistant could. She didn't dare look at Nelson; she didn't want to see the recrimination in his eyes. "Come on, Zeus, let's go."

Zeus got up without protest. "Thanks for hanging out with me," he muttered to Inez as Grace tugged him toward the exit. Inez didn't seem to hear. She was hissing something at her manager.

The security guard eyed them warily as they went out the front doors. Grace puffed out a relieved breath when they were out of his sight. "Zeus, remember that conversation we had about going too far?"

"I'm sorry, Gracie," Zeus mumbled.

She took one look at his distraught face and her frustration dissipated. "It's okay, Zuzu. I think I got enough for a story, anyway."

"Did you? Is it going to be all right?"

"It's going to be all right." Grace couldn't stop herself from thinking about Nelson, though. Even if he *had* liked her, he certainly didn't now.

She scoffed at herself. *Never dating again, remember? I was only there for the story.*

Zeus giggled, his gait taking on a distinctive strut. "I could write you a few stories if your article doesn't work out. Like the one about how I'm gonna diddle Inez Carter. It's a great story, with spaceships and laser guns and a killer dog that you think is the villain but it turns out he's really the hero."

Grace raised her eyebrows. "How do you think she's going to bang you? We just got kicked out of her recording session. And besides, Inez Carter is supposedly, like, twenty-four karat gay."

"She's gay for me, which means she's not gay. Unless I'm secretly hyper-reverse-gay. But I'm not. I'm actually a seagull." He flapped his arms like a bird, scuttling out in front and disappearing around the corner.

Grace watched after him thoughtfully. Inez once said in an interview that the only thing that disgusted her more than sex with men was "the bigot racist dipshit Nazis in congress, and people who fart on airplanes." But it *had* seemed like she'd been flirting with Zeus.

When Grace turned the corner, Zeus was standing stock still in the parking lot, staring at something. As she got closer, her stomach lurched: he was staring at the empty space where their car should have been.

"Did you activate the cloaking device?" he asked.

Grace groaned. "They towed it! God-fucking-dammit!"

He tsked. "You need to brush your teeth after language like that. Aren't you worried those words will give you gingivitis?"

Grace sat down heavily on the greasy asphalt and massaged her temples. Zeus got a faraway expression, tapping a finger on his lips. "I think that the fluoride in toothpaste is what spasms out people's brains and makes them curse. That way they spend more money on toothpaste and dentists to decontaminate their mouths. It's an international dental conspiracy."

Grace sighed heavily, then pulled out her cell and dialed the number on the towing sign.

"I mean, it makes sense, right?" Zeus continued. "Fluoride is an f-word, too, so it has a cosmic connection with the proverbial f-bomb, the ruler of all expletives. The connection allows them to transmit like a radio signal through your fillings. It all fits!"

"Hello?" Gracie said when someone answered. "No, I don't want to hold!" She gnashed her teeth as the line clicked and bad horn jazz began to play.

"Be careful what you tell them," Zeus said. "I think it's the dentists that towed your car. They want to slow us up now we're onto them." He paced back and forth, whispering to himself about flossing and retainers.

Grace hoped she had enough credit left to get her car out of impound. She winced and leaned back against the Mustang parked in the next space.

The air exploded in a cacophony of whoops and honks. Grace leapt up in a panic; it took her a couple heartbeats to realize she'd set off the Mustang's alarm.

Zeus's eyes went wide. "Ohmygod! That will bring the dentists down on us from all directions! We've got to scram!" He ran back down the sidewalk the way they'd come, his arms flailing.

Grace clutched her fingers in her hair. "Zeus, stop!" He either didn't hear or didn't care. She ran after him, trying to keep the phone against her ear. As the screech of the alarm diminished, she heard someone talking on the line.

"Hello?" a bored-sounding woman said. "Are you there?"

"I'm here. Zeus, STOP!" He was half a block ahead of her; he turned and said something she couldn't hear, then kept running.

"Excuse me?" the woman on the phone said.

"Sorry, I'm talking to someone else. Um, I believe you guys towed my car." She gave the woman her information, panting as she ran. She finally caught up with Zeus when he stopped in front of a bakery to count the polka dots on the display cake. Grace leaned against the wall and tried to catch her breath.

A computer keyboard clacked on the other end of the line. "One of our drivers was dispatched to that location, but he hasn't returned yet, so you're not entered in the system. He should be back in an hour or so."

Grace spat out a frustrated "thank you," jabbed the disconnect button, and pressed the heels of her hands into her eyes.

"It's twenty-one polka dots!" Zeus said, jumping up and down. "That's how many years old I am. That means we're supposed to buy this cake."

The bell dinged as he opened the bakery door, but Grace snagged his sleeve before he could go in. "Zeus, we don't have enough money to buy a cake. Besides, that one's made of Styrofoam."

He stared at her, a crease growing between his eyebrows. "Who would eat a Styrofoam cake? Is that some new diet fad? Is Styrofoam gluten-free?"

She tugged his sleeve. "Come on, Zuzu."

He let the bakery door close, giving the cake a forlorn look before following her. She opened her Lyft app, and was mentally calculating whether her credit card could withstand a ride charge along with the towing fee, when running footsteps approached from behind. "Wait!"

They turned, and Zeus broke into a wide grin. "Inez!"

The singer stopped, breathing hard and looking up at him through her long eyelashes. Zeus' eyes followed the progress of her breasts as they heaved.

"I didn't want you to leave," she said. "That engineer is a twatmonkey."

Zeus adopted a serious expression. "I've given the matter due consideration, and I think I shouldn't have thrown the noodle."

Inez twirled a lock of her bright cherry hair around her finger. "But anyway, I told those buttloafs I'm done for the day. You wanna go to a rave tonight?"

Zeus gasped. "Ohmygod, yes." He started making squeaky electronic noises and dancing enthusiastically. Passersby averted their eyes and gave him a wide berth.

Inez looked Grace up and down. "You can come, too, reporter girl."

"A *rave?*" Grace hadn't been to a rave since college, though Zeus had gone to a few. He loved them: he'd made a study of EDM, incorporating some of the beats into his guitar playing. Plus, they seemed to be a great place for him to meet people as bizarre as he was.

Zeus did a wild disco twirl and danced over to bump Inez's hip with his. "Please, Gracie? I wanna go to a rave, Gracie."

Grace studied Inez's pale, painted face. The cold-hearted reporter in her was curious to see how the story of the love affair between Zeus and the supposedly-gay rock star developed. But it would probably end with a brokenhearted Zeus, and that fact made her want to kick Inez Carter's ass. Hard. Like, you'd be able to eat cereal out of the dents in her butt cheeks afterwards.

Zeus seemed to sense Grace's struggle, and wiggled over to her, clasping his hands in front of him. "Pleeeeeease? Pretty, beautiful, gorgeous please? The please that launched a thousand ships and porn sites?"

Grace puffed out her cheeks. If she knew her foster son—and she did—he'd figure out a way to see the singer again, no matter what Grace did. And this was a chance to get a much more comprehensive story, maybe even an exclusive interview with Inez.

Grace needed a lucky break, *badly*. If she could get her freelancing career off the ground, she could go from being a loser who had ruined her life with bad choices, to a successful eccentric.

She shrugged. "Sure, we'll go to your rave. Why not?"

Zeus grabbed a giggling Inez by the hands and twirled her around. "Thanks, Gracie. You're more killer than a bucketful of killer whales."

"I sure am," she muttered.

There was another flurry of footsteps on the pavement, and they all turned to see a man scuttling up like a squirrel after a French fry. One of his shoelaces dragged on the pavement, and he clutched a cell phone in his stubby fingers. He came to a halt in front of Inez, gazing up at her raptly. "You're Inez Carter."

"I know," Inez said. She stared back at the young man in silence for a few moments as he smoothed his badly cut hair and wiped the sweat from his upper lip. "Do you want a photo with me?" Inez eventually asked.

The man laughed, a painfully embarrassing sound, like an accidental fart in public. Zeus backed away from him warily.

"Ohmygosh, yes," the guy said. "I'm sorry, I'm so nervous. I'm just such a huge fan of yours. You have no idea."

A wave of pity for the man washed over Grace. "I'll take the picture, if you want."

The man blinked at her with glassy eyes and held out his phone. It was warm and damp with sweat. Grace wiped it surreptitiously on her jeans before tapping the camera app and centering the man and Inez in the frame.

Inez smiled brightly and put her arm around him, without a hint of hesitation or disgust, which kicked her up a notch in Grace's estimation. The top of his head only came up to Inez's chin, and he stood stiffly in her embrace, smiling at the camera the way a madman would smile at an oncoming train. Grace began shooting photos immediately; there was no point in waiting for this guy to become photogenic.

"What's your name, anyway?" Inez asked.

"Me? Uh, Gary Euclid."

Inez smiled. "Nice to meet you, Uh Gary Euclid."

Grace handed the phone back to him. She'd taken about fifteen photos; all of them gave the impression that Gary was being mugged.

"Thank you," Gary squawked. He took a deep breath. "I-just-wanted-to-thank-you-for-all-you're-doing-for-the-LGBTQ-community. I've been picked on my whole life, and it means a lot when someone like you stands up and says, 'Hey, world, being gay is okay.'" He wiped his upper lip again, blinking rapidly.

Inez patted him on his hunched shoulder. "Being gay *is* okay, Gary Euclid. I'm okay, you're okay."

He grinned, showing about six acres of gums, and Grace thought to herself that being gay was the least of this guy's social problems.

"I've got to go now," Inez said. "I'll see you guys later." She winked theatrically at Zeus, then skipped back toward the studio, her pigtails swinging.

Grace and Zeus were locked in an awkward staring contest with Gary.

"Are you guys fans, too?" he asked, clutching his phone as if it might try to struggle out of his grasp.

"Yes," Zeus said. "What do you claim, bruh, oscillating or ceiling?"

Gary's broad, flat forehead creased slightly.

Zeus stuck out his arms and began twirling. "I'll turn on the fan and make it *cool* in here."

He whirled off down the sidewalk, and Grace smiled with uncomfortable pity at Gary, who stood licking his chapped and bulbous lips, his mildly perplexed gaze following Zeus as he spun away.

"Uh, it was nice meeting you," Grace said.

"Likewise," Gary said, then turned and stalked off the way he'd come.

Grace pulled at her lip, watching him go. Then she started after the still-whirling Zeus.

This town was a trip. If regular people on the street were as bizarre as Gary Euclid, Grace didn't even want to think what the ravers would be like.

Part of her wondered if Nelson would be at the party. She gave that part of her a swift kick in the ass.

4

Grace stood in the cramped office of the towing company, trying not to leap over the reception counter and wring the attendant girl's tattooed neck. "What do you mean, I owe you for two days' storage? My car isn't even here yet!"

The girl rolled her eyes, which were lined thickly enough to theoretically cover double shiners. "Our calendar day ends at 7:00 p.m. Since your car was in our custody from 5:45 to when it arrives…" She squinted out the window. The truck was just now pulling into the lot, Grace's little sedan dragging behind. "Right now, at 7:10, that's two days."

Grace's last nerve burst open like a kernel of popcorn. "I got here at 6:55. It's not my fault your driver decided to stop for a burger before coming in."

"Ma'am, our drivers are professionals. He wouldn't stop for a burger when he was on the clock. He got here as quick as he could."

Grace wanted to chew up the girl's "ma'am" and spit it back in her face.

The back door squeaked, and the tow truck driver came in, scratching his belly. "Hey, babe." He plopped a greasy paper sack down on the counter. "Got you a burger." He stretched out in the office chair, spinning lazily as he unwrapped his own.

Grace cocked an eyebrow at the girl, who stared back levelly. "Like I told you," the girl said, "the charge is $426.56. If you don't pay it now, it's just going to go up another $150 tomorrow at seven."

Grace fought back tears of frustration. She currently had $354.76 of credit left before her card was maxed out, and she had three more days until her unemployment check and Zeus's Social Security check came. "I want to see your manager," she said.

"The manager isn't available right now," the girl responded primly.

"My dad's the manager, and he's home today," the driver said, spitting crumbs. "His knee's acting up, they think it might need surgery."

Grace was wracking her brains for ideas on how to resolve this situation that didn't involve felony assault when the string of bells over the front door clanked sharply and Zeus burst into the room. "Gracie, I found an arrowhead." He held out his palm, displaying a pointed splinter of gravel. "See the marks from the stone hammer?"

"Zeus, I'm a little busy."

"There might be more artifacts here." He gazed brightly at the driver and attendant. "Can I use your shovel? Your good one. None of those off-brand ones with the floppy handles."

The tow truck driver stopped chewing, and the girl pursed her lips; Grace could see her wheels spinning as she tried to formulate the correct response. Zeus often had that effect on people. "I'm sorry," the girl said, a smile arranging itself awkwardly on her burgundy-painted lips. "We don't have a shovel."

"What do you mean, you don't have a shovel?" He craned his neck, trying to get a look through the doorway into the back room. "How could you even run an operation like this without a shovel? It looks distinctly greasy and mechanical in here. Can I have a look?"

He stepped around the reception counter. The driver pushed his wheeled chair back in alarm, and the girl's hands fluttered a moment in confusion before she leapt up to block Zeus' path. "Sir, you can't come in here."

"What are you guys hiding?" Zeus stared the girl down. "Are you aware that you built your offices over a historically important archaeological site? Are you trafficking in artifacts?"

The attendant threw a glance at the driver, who huddled in his chair, staring wide-eyed at the six-foot-three tower of well-muscled crazy that had suddenly invaded his space. He shrugged, giving his girlfriend a hopeless look.

The girl's lips drew into a tight line as she looked back at Zeus. "Sir, if you don't leave, I'm going to have to call the police."

"Oh, please do," Zeus said, flipping his curls back defiantly. "Ask for my father, Sargent Jared Ingrams. He'll be delighted to know what kind of business you're running here."

The girl froze. Her eyes darted between Zeus and Grace, obviously trying to work out if he was serious. Grace returned her gaze dispassionately, putting her hands on her hips.

"I think I should call my dad right now, in fact," Zeus said. "Gracie, can I use your phone?"

Grace fished her phone from her pocket and handed it to him, not taking her eyes off the girl. Zeus shoved the computer keyboard aside, sat on the desk, and started dialing.

Grace smiled sweetly at the girl. "Take $150 off that bill and I'll pay it. Then we'll get out of your hair."

"Hello?" Zeus said. "Sergeant Jared Ingrams, please. It's his son. Yes, I'll hold, but tell him it's important." His eyes found Grace's, and he gave a determined nod.

The girl scrambled to her computer, leaning as far away from Zeus as possible, and began printing off a new receipt. Grace paid the reduced amount and accepted the keys the girl stuffed into her hands. The driver watched the whole transaction in silence, chewing thoughtfully.

Grace put her hand on Zeus' shoulder. "Come on, Zuzu."

He didn't move, sitting stiffly on the desk. His brow was furrowed, his eyes distant as he pressed the phone to his ear. "What do you mean? His *son*. Oh, that's bullshit. He needs to acknowledge the fruit of his hard-working loins."

The girl looked on, and Grace could see comprehension catching hold. Grace tugged on Zeus's arm. "Come on. Let's *go*."

To her relief, he stood. "Are you calling me a liar?" he said into the phone as Grace pulled him out the door. "I don't appreciate this sort of treatment, especially from a man who refused to pay child support for eighteen years."

Grace shoved Zeus into the car and jumped into the driver's seat. The girl watched angrily through the window as they peeled out. Grace gave her a bright smile and waved goodbye.

"Oh, don't hang up on me," Zeus said. He huffed and jabbed the disconnect icon. "Can you believe that Gracie?" He started to dial again, but Grace snatched the phone from his hands.

"That guy isn't really your father, Zeus. He's just some cop that arrested you." She smiled to herself. The day after Mitch confessed he was having an affair, Zeus hung his car keys and wallet from the top of a radio tower. That was how they'd met Ingrams.

"Officer Ingrams said he wished he were my father, so he could give me a spanking," Zeus said. "I told him we had a deal, but apparently he wants to renege. It's not right, and I won't abide it. Give me back the phone, Gracie."

"No, Zeus." She pocketed her phone and eased into traffic.

"You're going to let that injustice stand?" Zeus's golden eyes flashed at the indignity. "You'll truly let a father turn his back on his own son, in the process allowing an evil antiquities-trafficking cartel to flourish? That's a huge amount of corruption, Gracie. If we don't stop it, it could poison the veins of society and lay the whole system low." He leaned over and tried to fish her phone out of her pocket.

She slapped his hands away. "I'll risk it. Society has made it this far, I'm sure it'll live another day."

He slid his fingers up her thigh on another expedition towards her pocket. "Your morals are truly skewed, Gracie."

She grabbed his hand and firmly placed it in his lap, giving him The Look. "I find it's a practical way to be. It's hard to get by in the world with your morals on completely straight. Now, let's go back to the motel and get cleaned up. We have a rave to go to."

A grin spread across Zeus's face. He started blowing a trance beat through his lips and dancing in his seat.

"That's more like it," Grace said.

Grace pawed through her half of the motel's rickety dresser, realizing that none of her clothes really screamed "rave." Most of them would be afraid to whisper it. With her current options, she could go the jeans-and-t-shirt route, or just keep the pantsuit on and try for a hip Hillary Clinton look.

She thought longingly of her old stage outfits moldering away in storage: thigh-high red suede boots, vintage '70s dresses, a neon green bridal gown…

She scowled and tugged her last clean t-shirt out of the drawer. *I'm too old for that stuff, anyway. Mitch was right, I should have thrown it all out.*

A thought struck her, and Grace froze with her arms through the t-shirt. Mitch was almost ten years older than her. Grace suspected he'd fallen in love with her because she was young and carefree: because she played in bands and represented all the things Mitch secretly resented missing out on in his youth. But as soon as they'd been married, he'd shamed her for her immaturity. He'd worked hard at changing her into someone she wasn't…and someone he wasn't interested in any longer. That accomplished, he'd traded her in for a younger model.

Grace yanked the t-shirt the rest of the way on, huffing. "Fuck that guy," she muttered.

She was going to have fun tonight. And, at her first opportunity, she was going to get some of her cool clothes out of storage.

Zeus came prancing out of the bathroom stark naked. He shook off his wet hair like a dog (a motion which had unfortunate Newtonian consequences for his exposed anatomy), stretched out on the carpet, and started doing sit-ups.

Grace shrieked and pulled the neck of her t-shirt over her eyes. "Zeus, what are you doing? Put some clothes on!"

"I will when I'm done. I need to see my ab muscles working, to make sure my form is correct. I don't want my six-pack to be all freaky lopsided."

She blundered into the bathroom with the shirt still over her face and turned on the shower, grateful that Zeus had cleared his fort out of the tub. By the time she got clean, rinsed out her eyes, and emerged from the bathroom, Zeus had, thankfully, donned jeans and a neon yellow t-shirt. He was dancing in front of the mirror, dozens of elaborate kandi bracelets rattling around his wrists and forearms.

He quit dancing and grabbed Grace by the still-damp hand. "Let's go, let's go, let's go."

"Hold on, I need to put on some makeup or something, and brush my hair."

"You're just as pretty without makeup, and let your hair get its freak on, like the rest of you. The only thing you need is some kandi." He slipped off a couple bracelets of neon plastic beads and slid them around her wrists, grinning maniacally. "It's a Hollywood rave!"

Grace glanced forlornly at her reflection in the mirror but relented. She was sure Nelson wouldn't be there, and even if he were, who was she kidding? It didn't matter what she looked like. A thirty-one-year-old woman living in a motel with someone like Zeus in tow was too much baggage even for a drummer like Nelson, who had a ten-piece kit.

Zeus sang loudly all the way down the stairs to the parking lot, then plugged his phone into her car's aux jack and pumped dubstep at top volume as they pulled out into traffic. He danced madly in his seat, his arms flailing wildly out his open window. Grace kept her eyes resolutely forward at stoplights, avoiding the glances of other drivers.

As they arrived in the hilltop neighborhood Inez had directed them to, Grace jabbed the stereo's power button, plunging them into abrupt silence.

Zeus' eyes bugged out with indignity. "Hey! I need music to prepare my soul for this experience." He turned it back on.

Grace turned it off, again. "Zeus, the people who live here will have the help call in a noise complaint if you don't chill out." The sprawling mansions slid by in the golden twilight, watching Grace's beat-up Honda with their noses in the air. She double-checked the address on her map app. "Is this really where they're going to have a rave?"

"Of course. This is where they're going to have the best rave ever. These people know how to get drugs we've never even heard of."

Grace almost choked. "Drugs? Wait, you don't do rave drugs, do you, Zeus? I thought you just went to these things for the musical experience."

Zeus blinked uncomprehendingly. "Drugs *are* part of the musical experience, Gracie. I thought you knew that. You're a musician and everything."

Panic crawled down Grace's scalp. "No drugs, Zeus. For the love of God. You don't think you're crazy enough when you're sober?"

He just stared at her and turned the music back on. There was a short struggle that Grace won, prying the phone out of his hands and unplugging it from the aux. In the process, her car swerved into the path of an oncoming Bentley.

Zeus let out a yelp, clutching his seat. Grace jerked the car back into her lane just before their bumpers made contact. The Bentley passed by, the driver scowling at her wide-eyed through the window.

Grace's heart pounded in her throat. An accident was the last thing she needed. For one, she suspected her cheap insurance was actually a money laundering operation for the Sinaloa cartel.

When she'd called them to change her address, a guy had answered sounding like he was still in bed. "*Bueno?* Oh yeah, yeah, the insurance thing, right, let me get a pen…"

They'd probably call out a hit on her rather than pay a claim.

Grace's heart was just starting to find its normal rhythm when her phone buzzed in her jeans pocket. She pulled onto the narrow shoulder of the winding road and pulled it out.

She stared at the screen. Lawrence again. He couldn't expect a story this fast, could he? She punched the answer button, hoping he wasn't trying to make good on her promise of a date already. "Hello?"

"Hi, Grace."

His voice was flat, and Grace's stomach went hollow. "What's up?"

"Just calling you to tell you not to bother with that story. Marla Poccino got it in already."

Grace's tongue stuck to the roof of her mouth; she had to pry it off. "She got a story? But…she couldn't have been in the studio more than a few minutes!" She cursed. Zeus was watching her, his expression suddenly solemn.

"I'm sorry," Lawrence said. "I didn't even call her. I don't know how she got the lead."

Yeah, whatever. Marla was a well-respected freelancer, while Grace was a complete unknown. Lawrence had probably called Marla first, and then Grace out of pity. "Thanks, Lawrence," she sighed.

"I'll call you on the next one, don't worry, and it will probably be even better."

She winced at his bracing tone and wondered if he really would. "Yeah. Thanks, again."

She hung up and stared blankly at her lap.

Zeus fidgeted in his seat. "That ugly chick with the freckles stole your job?"

"Yeah." Grace blinked back sudden tears of helplessness.

Zeus put his arm around her shoulders. "Don't worry about it, Gracie. We're gonna make it, you'll see. The Universe farts on you sometimes just for fun, but that just makes it smell even better when it doesn't."

She tried to smile. "Yeah."

He ruffled her hair. "Now come on, let's go to the party and forget about it."

She wiped her eyes and grimaced. "I'm sorry, Zeus, but I don't really feel like going now."

He shook his head decisively. "Don't be irrunk-udunkulous. You need a party now more than ever. Besides, Inez will be there, and maybe some other shiny famous people. I bet they'll do something epic and you can write about it and get an even better story."

She gazed at him uncertainly. Maybe he was right. Was her luck that good?

Even if it wasn't, she could use a drink.

"Come on," Zeus urged, poking her in the ribs. "Let's go show those losers how to live."

She heaved a sigh and put the car in gear. "Okay."

Zeus clapped his hands and started dancing again as they headed back down the street, doing his weirdest moves, trying to make her laugh.

After another quarter mile, he pointed at a gated drive. "This is it, Gracie. The code for the gate is 6969."

"Clever." She pulled up alongside the keypad and entered the code. The gate slid smoothly open.

She sat frowning at it. Part of her had believed the code wouldn't work, that Inez had been playing some sort of prank on them.

Zeus nudged her shoulder with his knuckles. "Hurry, Gracie, let's go, before all the best cosmic narratives are gone!"

"Will do."

She drove up a wide lane flanked with cypress trees and parked in the circular drive. A three-story, old-world-style stone house rose before them. There were about two dozen other cars parked at haphazard angles in front of it.

Grace gazed at the place in awe. *I'll bet Marla Poccino isn't partying at a place like this tonight.* She pushed back the subsequent thought that the other freelancer was probably home eating a hot meal—prepared on a real stove, not a tiny microwave with a menacing hum that threatened imminent explosion.

Grace and Zeus climbed out of the car into the balmy twilight. Music thumped faintly behind the demure splash of a tiered fountain. "I guess this is the right place," she muttered, running her fingers through her uncombed ringlets. She glanced down at herself; her $19.99 sneakers had ketchup stains on them, and there was a hole in her t-shirt.

When she looked back up, Zeus was already at the front door, dancing in elaborate tecktonics as he rang the bell. Grace jogged up behind him just as the door opened.

A pimple-faced kid gazed out at them with wide, glassy eyes. He had multicolored strands of kandi sheathing both wrists. Fuzzy neon orange leggings encased his skinny calves. Behind him, the music thumped, along with the sound of many voices.

Zeus kept dancing, twirling and undulating his arms. "Hey, we're Zeus and Gracie," he said. "Inez Carter invited us."

The kid surveyed them, his grin spreading so wide Grace worried it would rupture some of his more dangerous-looking pimples. "Neat," he said, stepping aside. "Come in."

Zeus danced past him and Grace followed into a high-ceilinged foyer. A guy with scruffy blond hair lay on his belly on the flagstones, drawing shapes in what appeared to be his own spit. A girl sat cross-legged beside him, droning out a Gregorian chant.

Zeus would fit in just fine here.

"My name's Rolland," the pimple-faced kid said, still staring at her with that jaw-twisting grin. "This is my friend Nicholson's house. His parents are in Morocco right now."

"That's cool," Grace mumbled, uncomfortably aware that she was likely closer to the age of those absent parents than to their child. Should she stomp in and order all these kids home to bed? That's what a responsible adult would do.

But turning thirty hadn't brought Grace any closer to being a responsible adult. All it had done was burden her with a creeping notion that she *should* be progressing in that direction.

A boy dashed through the foyer, giggling and twirling lighted spheres on a string. A girl chased after him, playing a ukulele and singing, "Purple is my favorite song, I hope you all will sing along." She looked familiar, and Grace realized she'd seen her on the cover of *Rolling Stone*. Her name was Lyssa Medlin, an up-and-coming indie artist.

All notions of adulthood vanished in a puff of skunky smoke. Grace and Zeus exchanged a glance, and she knew they were both thinking the same thing: they'd somehow been invited to the coolest party in Hollywood.

5

She couldn't hear a word the guy was saying over the music, but that was probably for the best. His black-hole pupils swallowed the flashing lights on the dance floor, and his slack smile barely moved despite his constant stream of narrative. His electric blue drink smelled poisonously alcoholic, though with his hairless, round cheeks and shining doe-eyes, he looked about fifteen.

The kid grabbed her hand and tugged her toward the dance floor, almost making her spill her own drink. "Let's make dream sandwiches," she thought she heard him say.

Grace resisted for a moment, then shrugged. She took a generous gulp of her cocktail—her third—and followed him into the twitching morass of dancers.

She had no idea how to do the freakish dances of those around her, so she just stood tapping her foot to the beat, trying her best to stay out of people's way. She hoped for a glimpse of a celebrity, preferably one doing something dangerous or illegal, but Lyssa Medlin was nowhere to be seen and Grace didn't see anyone else she recognized. The booze was beginning to buzz in her head, though, and she only half-cared. It felt good to think about something other than journalism and her desperate attempt to put her life back together, if only for one evening.

She wondered again if Nelson was coming. She downed the rest of her drink to push that thought out.

Grace felt something rubbing against her knee and looked down. The zonked-out boy now seemed to be humping her leg. She took a startled step back, directly into a flailing, many-armed beast of dancers; it didn't seem to notice, but just writhed away on an altered trajectory.

A hand grabbed her arm, and she turned to see Zeus glaring and shaking a finger at her dance partner. "No! Bad dog!"

The boy gave Grace a hurt look as Zeus led her away. She felt a little sorry for him. Hopefully, he'd find a more amenable leg to hump before the night was through.

Zeus took her to the makeshift bar, where a guy that looked like Lenny Kravitz refilled Grace's cup with haphazard splashes of alcohol and blue Kool Aid, throwing in a few gummy bears for good measure.

Zeus just got the Kool Aid. Of all his many faults and quirks, drinking wasn't one: he said alcohol smashed the windshield of his brainmobile.

They went out into the hallway, which was a bit quieter, even considering the girl lying on the floor reciting a long list of potato products while her friend meowed like a cat.

Grace smiled at them and gave them a nod of greeting, but they didn't respond. This crowd was the weirdest Grace had ever seen, and that was saying something.

Zeus smoothed Grace's hair fussily. "You okay? That pork pie get anything on you?"

"I'm fine, Thanks for saving me, Zuzu. Have you seen Inez?"

"I haven't seen Inez, but she exists, I just know it." He slurped down his Kool Aid and dropped the empty cup on the floor. Then he slapped his palms against the wall one after the other, making a suck-pop noise each time. "Now, I'm going to climb this wall like one of those gooey-skinned tree frogs."

His feet scrabbled against the wainscoting, and he fell over backwards, his eyes wide with surprise as he hit the ground.

The meowing girl stopped meowing, and glanced at him. "You all right?"

"Tater tots," her friend said. "Potato starch. Potato gun."

"I'm fine," Zeus said, getting back up again. "I guess my suction bladder isn't working correctly today."

"I meow it when that happens, meow," the girl said, her eyes glazing back over.

"Baked potato. Perogies. McDonalds apple pie."

Grace took a sip of her drink, wincing at the strong combination of absinthe and candy. "Having a good time, Zeus?"

He nodded decisively. "There is so much good time in here that I'm saving some in my pockets for later, in case we run out." They grinned at each other. He grabbed her hand. "Come on. I hear they've got cake upstairs."

Grace's ears perked. "They have food in this place?"

"Of course they have food. You have to fuel up the freak machine sometimes."

They plowed through a group of people having Slinky races on the stairs and gained the kitchen, which was four times the size of their motel room. Laid out on the white marble countertops was a stoner smorgasbord. Grace passed over the cake, since a guy currently had his face buried in it, but found a slice of pizza that looked safe. Zeus carefully carved some cake from around the man's forehead and headed toward a pan of brownies.

"Zeus, don't," Grace said, examining the suspicious green chunks in the chocolate. "I don't think those are the regular kind."

Zeus shrugged. "I'm not the regular kind, either."

Grace grabbed his arm. "Seriously."

"Fuck!" a voice from the doorway exclaimed. A girl with screamingly red hair stumbled into the room, fell onto the granite tiles, and slid three feet before ramming into the kitchen island.

Another girl ran over and knelt at her side, her dark eyes shining with concern. She was wearing Day-Glo yellow pants embroidered with rocket ships of cut crystal.

An elaborate florescent-green ruff hemmed them just below the knee. Grace couldn't look away from them: they were the most fabulous pants she'd ever seen, and she immediately knew they could be worn by none other than Nicole Watters, better known as BeatBot.

"Inez, are you okay?" Nicole said.

"That floor is fucked," came the muffled answer.

"Inez!" Zeus cried, spitting brownie crumbs everywhere. He jumped over and helped her up, which looked like no easy task; the singer swayed and flailed on limp legs before gaining an upright status.

"That was a kickass nosedive you took," Zeus said. "You were all, browwwwrrr BOOSH!" He laughed. "Are you drunk? You're drunk, right?"

Inez grinned woozily, clinging to his arm. "I'm not even drunk. I only had like, three, five…some weird number of lemon drops at the bar." She giggle-snorted.

Nicole stood off to the side, watching the interaction with a slight frown.

"You shouldn't involve yourself with weird numbers," Zeus said. "It can interfere with the gravitational physics." He reached for the brownie pan, grabbing another huge slice.

"Zeus," Grace said, catching his wrist. "No."

Zeus gave her a nonplussed look. "It's just a little bit of weed, and what's a little bit of weed after the huge amount of LSD I ingested? It'll just slightly torque the rails."

Grace's stomach plummeted. "You took *acid?* Zeus, oh my God, what…what the fuck were you thinking?" She had to get him out of here. She didn't even want to think about the disruptive phenomenon Zeus would be on hallucinogens.

He just stared at her. "What do you mean? You've taken about twice as much as me. I thought you were down. I thought it was party time."

Grace scowled. "I haven't taken any acid."

A slow grin spread across his face, and he laughed. "Oh, boink, Gracie. You didn't know? Never drink the electric Kool Aid at a rave if you don't want to get ker-plipped."

All the blood drained from Grace's body. "There's acid in the Kool-Aid?"

"Of course there's acid in the Kool Aid." Zeus started to giggle, and Inez joined in, leaning against him.

Grace tugged at her hair. She hadn't taken acid in…how long had it been? More than a flippin' decade. She was too fucking *old* for this.

Nicole gave Grace a look of frank compassion. "You okay?"

She blew out a puff of air. "I hope so."

"Hey, it's Grace," a familiar voice said, and Grace's gaze jerked toward it. *Shit. Not now.* Nelson leaned against the arched entryway, grinning. "How are you?" he asked.

Grace broke out in a cold sweat. Her skin started to crawl. "I feel weird."

The smile dropped off Nelson's face. "Everything okay?"

Nicole came over and laid a hand on her shoulder. "You're going to be all right."

Zeus giggled again, stuffing another hunk of brownie into his mouth. "You're gonna transcend all right, Gracie."

6

They found a bench under the corkscrewing, flower-tufted canopy of a tree in the backyard. Nelson sat next to Grace, and Zeus plopped down at her feet. Inez wandered off to puke in a lavender bush while Nicole held her hair.

The last smoggy glow of sunset hovered over the twinkling lights of the city, which moved like reflections on undulating shards of mirror. Grace puffed out a breath and wiped the cold sweat from her brow.

Nelson smirked. "You feeling it?" The garden flowed around him like liquid. The tree branches twined and danced to a tinny melody Grace realized was the sound of Inez retching in the bushes.

"I'm feeling it," Grace said.

Nelson laughed. His beard had an opalescent sheen, and she could see every pore on his nose, but she liked looking at his face. She smiled back.

"I haven't taken acid in years," he said, a bit wistfully. "Maybe I should go get some of that Kool Aid for myself. Then we can be whacked out together."

Grace grinned wider, her jaw stretching out until she pictured herself as Jack Nicholson. Then she glanced down at Zeus, who was staring intently at her hand, tracing her knuckles with a blade of grass.

Her smile faded. "I can't get whacked out. I have to keep it together so I can look after *him*."

Nelson watched Zeus thoughtfully, tugging his fingers through his beard. "He'll be okay. No one here cares if he gets a bit goofy. In fact, he'd stick out if he didn't." They glanced over at a boy who was blowing farty blasts on a trumpet, chasing a poor cat from one bush to the next. Over at the pool, people were racing boats made of folded beer cartons while a rival army tried to sink them with bottle rockets.

"Yeah," she said. "But…"

Nelson laid a hand on her shoulder. "If you're really worried about it, I'll stay sober and sane. I'll look after him, okay? I'll look after both of you."

Nelson's warmth seeped into her shoulder and flowed through her bloodstream. "You don't have to do that," she said.

"I want to. I don't want you to worry."

Zeus's chin jerked up. He smiled at Grace toothily, strange glints in his eyes. "He's right. Stop worrying so much. We're gonna have a good time." He sprang to his feet and leapt into the tree, the branches rustling as he scrambled up the trunk and disappeared into the leaves.

"Grrrrr," he said. "Rawr."

Grace caught Nelson's eye, rubbing her nose nervously. "You really think you're up for babysitting?"

He laughed. "Sure." A strange look passed over his face. "That's basically my job, anyway."

Grace's brow furrowed. "What was that?"

"Nothing." Nelson glanced over at Inez. She had finished puking and was kneeling in the grass, coaxing the twilight moths toward her with airy gestures. "Come to mama," Inez said, but the moths continued to flutter serenely around the lavender, their insect-minds obviously on something else. The singer scowled. "Come see your fucking mother, you ungrateful shits." Nicole stood beside her, staring off at the view and frowning.

A voice rang out from the direction of the house. "There you guys are." A man in baggy shorts and a neon pink t-shirt strode toward them, flashing a polished grin. Neon yellow sunglasses were propped in his slickly disheveled hair and a single strand of pink and yellow kandi encircled his wrist. He looked like a 45-year-old man dressed up in a rave kid costume as a joke, and Grace started to laugh before she realized that it probably wasn't a joke: the man was Karma Korn's manager. She cleared her throat.

"Hey, Duke," Nelson said, reaching out to shake his hand. "How's it going?"

"Great, great, super awesome." Grace found herself mesmerized by the unnatural straightness and whiteness of Duke's teeth. "You all having a good time tonight?" he asked.

Grace nodded nervously, trying to meet his eyes, but unable to look away from his teeth. He looked like an ageing hipster nutcracker doll.

"We're partying like it's 1999," Nelson said, shooting Grace an amused glance. She snorted.

Duke barked with laughter. "Yeah, I went to a lot of great parties in 1999. Or at least I assume I did, since I can't remember most of them." He laughed again.

Grace strained her jaw with a smile. Nelson stroked his beard, nodding thoughtfully. Inez finally looked away from her moths. "Why are you here, Duke? Do you want to make sure that I'm, like, partying in the right way? That I'm projecting the correct branding image?"

Duke gave her a double blast from his finger guns. "Oh, you."

A laugh threatened to boil over in Grace's mouth like scalding milk.

Another man popped out of the shadows, and Grace's laugh turned into a squeak of fear. It was Duke's assistant from the studio, dressed all in black, his eyes shining like evil elfstones in his angular face.

"Ah, here's Tristan," Duke said. "Liking the party?" He patted him on the back, and Tristan cringed away slightly, hunching his shoulders.

"It's fine," Tristan said, as if it were the seventeenth time Duke had asked. His eyes darted to Grace's, and she shuddered.

Nelson stood up. "Come on, party animals. Why don't we go inside and get some pizza?"

Grace stood on legs that felt like helium balloons. Inez lurched to her feet, helped by Nicole.

"I already had dinner at this great little restaurant by my house," Duke said. "I should take you all there sometime, actually. They have this fried guinea hen with taro root puree. I really shouldn't put pizza on top of that. What the heck, though, right?" He patted his taut stomach. "Calories don't count at a party."

They all stared at him in bewildered silence for a moment, except for Tristan, who just loomed sullenly.

"My God, Duke, you are such a frigging square," Inez said.

Nelson roused himself and clapped his hands. "Let's get some pizza."

"Can I bring the moths with me?" Inez asked.

"Of course," Nelson said.

She stomped her foot. "Moths! Come inside! Pizza!"

Grace half expected the insects to comply, but they didn't.

"I don't want pizza," Zeus' voice declared from inside his rustling cocoon of branches. "Tigers don't eat pizza. Tigers eat sika deer and chital. Is there any of that?"

"We can check," Nelson said.

The branches creaked as Zeus jumped out of the tree and loped over, growling.

They started toward the house, but Inez didn't follow. Instead she began to cry, tears streaking through her thick eyeliner. "Why won't they come? Why don't the moths love me anymore?"

Nelson stopped and sighed. "They do. But part of love is knowing when to let go."

Inez sniffed heavily. "But I *want them with me*. I'm *nothing without them*."

"You're plenty, even without them," Nelson said.

"You have a whole teeming psychic wonderland inside your skull," Zeus said. "There are imagination moths in there, and you can carry them with you everywhere, so you don't need to burden yourselves with the real ones. Rawr. Hissss."

Inez smeared her mascara as she wiped her eyes. "Really?"

"Rrrrrealy," Zeus said.

"It's true," Nelson said.

Inez permitted herself to be led back into the house. Zeus trailed behind, swiping his claws at unseen enemies, and Grace followed, her head billowing behind her like a cloak.

She glanced back at Nicole, who was staring at her feet as she walked, tapping out a rhythm on her thighs. Grace tried to reassemble her normal self out of the pile of goo the acid had melted her into. Her original plan of getting an exclusive interview with Inez and Nicole now seemed distant and bizarre, but she had to at least try. "Some party, eh?" she said. "Hopefully I don't get so high I turn into an animal, too."

Nicole glanced up, blinking, then flashed the beautiful smile Grace had seen in publicity photographs. "Don't worry. If you do, we won't sell you to the zoo." Her smile faded, her hands tapping again, and Grace chewed her lip. Then she realized her lip felt like a big, rubbery truck tire, so she stopped.

The kitchen was deserted. In fact, it looked like it had been cleared out by an invading army. Cake was smeared across the floor amongst a litter of paper plates and pizza boxes. The empty pan of brownies had been overturned, and there were half-eaten cookies and half-drunk cups of Kool-Aid everywhere.

Duke glanced around at the carnage with ill-hidden disgust. "Whoa! Someone had some fun in here! I hope they have a good maid." He wandered out of the kitchen. To Grace's relief, his sinister assistant followed. Nicole, with a hopeless glance at Inez, went down the stairs to the dance party.

Somehow Nelson managed to locate an unsullied slice of pizza and began coaxing it into Inez. Zeus, meanwhile, had decided he was now an orangutan, and was knuckling around, hooting and digging through the debris.

Grace found herself drawn to the oversized, stainless-steel fridge. It was covered in magnets, and one caught her attention. It depicted a young woman with a bright, businesslike smile standing against a backdrop of blooming wisteria. The caption read, "Lacey Miles, Massage The rapist."

Grace's brow scrunched. Her lips moved as she read the words over and over. "Massage The rapist." She tried to make the caption jive with the photo, and the more she looked at it, the tighter the woman's smile seemed, skull-like, her eyes glittering with manic anger. "Massage the rapist!" the woman screamed through clenched teeth.

"No!" Grace said. "I don't want to!"

"Grace," Nelson said.

Grace looked up from the magnet and found Nelson locked in a struggle with Inez, who was attempting to drink a discarded cup of electric Kool-Aid. "Massage therapist," Grace said, the words finally clicking into place.

Nelson blinked at her. He was holding the cup out of Inez' reach as she stomped on his toes. "A little help?"

Grace shook her head to clear it. "Of course." She wrapped her arms around the young woman's bony torso and pulled. The smell of Inez' musky perfume mixed with stale vodka made Grace's nostrils sweat.

"Stop being Nazis!" Inez protested. "A woman has a right to her own body!" She was flailing so wildly that Grace momentarily thought she was wrestling the Kraken and had to shake her head to clear it again.

Then Grace realized it was far too quiet in the kitchen. "Where's Zeus?"

Inez's elbow caught her in the hip. Nelson, who had dumped the contents of all the half-empty cups into the sink, grabbed the struggling girl's wrists. "Got her."

Grace stepped away, smoothing her clothes. Inez's struggles were weakening, and Nelson had no trouble holding her now. "Fuzzy wuzzy wuzzy," the singer muttered, running the fabric of Nelson's flannel shirt between her fingers. Her eyelids sagged, and she laid her cheek on his shoulder.

"Where's Zeus?" Grace repeated.

Nelson glanced around at the empty kitchen, frowning. "I don't know."

The thump of music from downstairs ceased abruptly, replaced by the sound of angry voices.

A sick feeling ricocheted through Grace's acid-addled stomach. "Shit! Goddammit, Zeus!" She ran for the stairs, skidding slightly in the spilled cake, the world blending into a streak of tracers.

"Grace, wait!" Nelson called after her. "You don't know if he has anything to do—"

"It's him."

She tore open the door for the stairwell, which was full of people, all of them looking down toward the commotion. Their bodies felt like they were made of water balloons as she pushed through them. The handrail melted in her palm.

At the foot of the stairs, Grace could hear the angry voices more clearly. "Get the fuck down from there! Oh, my fucking God, my parents are gonna castrate me."

"They can't cut off what you don't have."

Grace winced. It was Zeus's voice.

She waded through the crowd on the dance floor. Everyone's gaze was fixed on a point above their heads, various expressions of amused incredulity twisting their waxy-looking faces.

"Who the fuck is this guy? Brett, help me get him down."

"I'm not going up there. No way. I don't even know how to get up there."

Grace finally broke through to the front where she could see what was happening. Nicole was behind the DJ booth, staring toward the ceiling with a concerned expression.

Grace thought the acid and flashing lights must be turning the shadows into something that wasn't there. Zeus was hanging upside down by his knees from the oversized, wrought-iron chandelier, holding an electric guitar in his hands. His fingers moved as he played silently, ignoring the commotion below. Grace's esophagus filled with bile.

A boy with bright pink hair gazed up at Zeus, a look of cold fury on his aristocratic features. "That's my dad's autographed Gibson. It's priceless now that B.B. King is dead. Get the fuck down, or I'm calling the cops."

There were outbursts of dismay from around the room.

"What am I supposed to do?" the pink-haired boy insisted. "I'm not supposed to be having this party at all, and if something happens to that guitar, I'm Texas toast."

There were more yells of protest, and people commanding Zeus to come down, and a confusion of partygoers pushing for the exit.

Tears sprang to Grace's eyes. Zeus grinned gleefully, seemingly unaware of anything except how fun it was to swing above the heads of the crowd.

"Zeus," she said. "Come down. Please." Her voice seemed weak and reedy amongst the noise. He didn't glance her way.

Grace felt suddenly very small, and very alone. That young man up there was her only real friend. But was he really her friend? There were dark moments in which she wondered if he had the capacity to truly care. If he did, he wouldn't do things like this, completely ruining her chances at salvaging a story and at building any sort of a good reputation in this town.

Her career was definitely over now. What had she been thinking, coming to this party? She was an old woman, deluding herself into believing she still had any relevance in the hip world.

Then Zeus's eyes caught hers, and he grinned. She saw the glint of mischief, and realized he wasn't unaware of the commotion. He was never unaware of anything.

Grace couldn't keep herself from smiling back. He did care. He may have just destroyed what was left of her life, but he hadn't meant to: he just had other priorities. And who could blame him? Making money was boring, and it crushed your soul.

Man, I'm too high, she thought. But she had to admit, she sorta had a point.

Zeus fiddled with something at the end of the guitar: he was plugging in a cord. Nicole jumped as a pop and squeal of feedback blasted from her speakers. Somehow, Zeus had found a way to patch the Gibson into the stereo system. He had a knack for figuring stuff like that out.

He started to play.

The mass exodus stopped, and people turned to watch. His fingers crawled across the fretboard, filling the room with noise. Somehow, with one instrument, he managed to make as much music as Beatbot had with all her samples and beats and gadgetry.

At first, it was beautiful noise chaos, but a rhythm grew out of it, and a melody, the song enveloping Grace and holding her transfixed. People started screaming again, but now they were cheering Zeus on. A lot of them resumed dancing. The pink-haired boy, who could only be Nicholson, the son of the owners of this place, was still staring up at Zeus, but the look of fury had been replaced by one of disbelief.

Zeus crafted an impossibly good song out of nothing as he swung back and forth on his knees, making the chandelier sway. His song's hook was completely nonderivative, and perfect enough to make Grace's scalp tingle. The chord progression was complex, so clever that it made Grace bust up in giggles, but he made it sound simple and natural. It wasn't until Zeus caught her eye again and broke out in a wide grin that she realized she was smiling like a maniac.

He pursed his lips at her in an exaggerated rock-n-roll face and played the final chords, letting them squeal. As they died away, the crowd broke out in cheers, stomping for more.

Zeus swung himself upright and dropped to the ground, the guitar held gently in one hand. He gave it to Nicholson, who looked at it like he'd never seen it before.

People pressed forward to mob Zeus, patting him on the back, giving him hugs, but he ambled through them to stand before Grace with his hands in his pockets.

He broke into a beatific grin. "I'm so high right now."

Grace laughed, tears rolling down her face. "That was awesome. But you're so stupid." She smacked him on the shoulder. "Why do you do things like that?"

He shrugged. "Even orangutans like to play guitar sometimes."

Grace raised an eyebrow.

There was a streak of movement. Zeus's eyes went wide as Inez crashed into him, pressing her lips to his in a drunken kiss. Nicole, still standing in the DJ booth, looked on with a hurt expression.

Duke appeared out of the crowd and pulled Inez away, leaving Zeus looking ruffled but pleased with himself.

Duke whispered something in Inez's ear, his expression livid.

Inez scowled. "Fuck that. Why should I care about that shit anymore? I'm famous now."

He said something else to her in a low voice, his lips moving like fleshy jackhammers. Tristan, the emo vampire assistant, came up alongside them, and then it was the three of them in an intense, whispered conversation.

Grace wondered if it was some sort of football huddle about Inez's correct comportment strategy to win the rock star Super Bowl. *LA is freaking weird.*

Inez broke away. "Whatever!" She stalked off, pushing her way through the crowd.

Grace glanced again at Nicole, who caught Grace looking and busied herself with her equipment. She quickly dropped the next beat and started the party again.

Zeus stood stroking his chin. People were still manhandling him and gushing about his guitar playing, but he barely seemed to notice. He frowned at Grace. "Is this how girls usually act?"

<h1 style="text-align:center">7</h1>

Grace navigated the nearly-empty streets back to the motel, squinting to get the stoplights to stop dancing. Dawn tinged the horizon with an electric glow, and her nerves were sizzling and shorting out.

Zeus hummed a tune under his breath as he shot finger guns at the shuttered bodegas. "BUHGOOOSH!" He mimed the billowing fireball with his hands then resumed humming, sighting his next target.

"Fuck, I wish I hadn't been so high," Grace moaned. "I spent my entire conversation with Nicole imitating electronic keyboard noises, when I should have been finding out what's fishy about her and Inez's relationship."

Zeus went abruptly still. "Don't use the word *fishy*." He took the hem of his shirt and vigorously wiped off his tongue. "Gahhhhh. Gahhh." Then he took a deep breath, squared his shoulders, and resumed his imaginary destruction of the neighborhood. "KERBOOOO!"

Grace gave him a long, sidewise glance, which he seemed deliberately unaware of. She cleared her throat. "I mean, how come Inez hits on you when she's a lesbian? Right in front of her girlfriend? And why does Nicole put up with it?"

Zeus shrugged, blowing smoke from the barrel of his finger gun. "Love is a team sport sometimes. BOOSH!"

"It's a pretty weird love triangle, you have to admit."

"It's more like a love Mobius strip. KEHBLOOO!"

Grace snorted. "Anyway, I didn't get much of a story, but at least my reputation isn't totally ruined. You seemed to make quite an impression, actually. If I hadn't been so orbital, I could have made some connections."

"It's good to make connections so that you have something to attach your ropes to when climbing the cliff of life. WHUBUSHHHHHH!"

Grace frowned as she pulled into the trash-strewn parking lot of their motel and cut the engine. She sat gazing at the sinuous crack in the grubby windshield. It glistened like a seam of diamond. Her brain was shrinking back to its normal size, or even smaller, shriveling like a fig. She'd hate herself in the morning for acting like an immature idiot and missing so many opportunities.

She felt Zeus's eyes on her and looked over to find him regarding her with a tiny smile. "That Lyssa Medlin chick, the one with that circus song they play rapid-fire on Spotify? She heard me play guitar," he said.

Grace smiled, trying not to crack her face, which felt like it was coated in a layer of sticky wax. She rubbed her tired eyes. "Yeah? That's cool. I'll bet she was impressed."

"She was, in fact. She asked me to come to her practice space tomorrow afternoon. I mean this afternoon, actually. She might want me in her band."

Grace took her hands from her face. "Really? Lyssa Medlin?"

He nodded.

Grace giggled and bounced in her seat. "Zeus, that's so awesome!"

"You can come with me to the practice. Maybe I can get her to hijack an airplane with me, and you can write a story about it. Maybe she'll even hijack it naked, which is even a super duper better story." He pulled at his bottom lip, his gaze turning inward, his lips curling in a blitzed-out smile. "Working those airplane controls with her…." He giggled.

"I don't even need to get a story out of it," Grace said. "It's just awesome. It's about time someone else saw how brilliant you are."

Zeus came out of his daydream and studied her face. "It's way past time for someone else to see how brilliant *you* are."

"Thanks, Zeus. That's sweet."

"It's not sweet, it's just true." He opened his door. "Now, come on, let's try to force our way into dreamland before they close it down. We've got to be sharp today, or we'll miss the schmooze train."

They emerged from the dirty car into the cool, predawn air, and traipsed up to their little room. Grace realized it had been their home for almost three weeks now. When she unlocked the door, the place looked even crappier than usual, glazed over by the cheap veneer of her acid crash.

Dull hopelessness seeped in through every pore as she flopped onto her lumpy bed. She was thirty-one years old and living in a motel. She couldn't even manage to land a stupid celebrity gossip story, and her best friend was a twenty-one-year-old who aspired to be a tiger when he grew up.

But at least she did have a best friend. How would she feel if she lost him? What if he got the success he deserved and took off on tour with Lyssa's band, leaving her alone?

She buried her face in her pillow. She should be *glad* if Zeus made it on his own. Clinging to him because of her own loneliness and inadequacies was *sick*. He had his own life, the whole of it still ahead of him. He didn't deserve to be shackled to a decrepit old ship as it sank.

"Come on, Gracie," Zeus said. "Don't flop down like a mudfish. Let's take a shower."

She snorted into her pillow, then looked up to find him grinning like a car salesman. "Look at Mr. Tomcat. All these girls drooling on you has made you cocky."

He glanced nervously at his clothing. "Did they drool on me? Gross." He clutched his hands in front of him, avoiding her eyes. "You like Nelson, right? I saw you guys making cutsie-eyes at each other, your hearts boing-boinging out of your chests and stuff."

Grace's sticky cheeks heated up, but they cooled off again when she saw Zeus' expression. "What's up, Zuzu? Why would that bug you?"

He sniffed, still having trouble meeting her gaze. "No. No. I'm just wondering about the topography of the landscape."

She studied him closely, her brow furrowing. "You're not *jealous,* are you Zeus? I mean, come on-"

"It's not that," he said quickly. "It's just, you know…" He scuffed the carpet with his feet. "Never mind." He wandered into the bathroom and shut the door.

Grace watched after him, chewing her lip. Maybe he was just as worried as she was about losing his best friend.

When her alarm went off at two that afternoon, Grace pried her gummy eyes open to find the world looking pretty much normal again, all of the LSD magic gone save for a faint, rainbow halo around the grimy motel furniture.

She shut off the alarm, then groaned slightly as the previous evening's events crept into her brain like a gang of vandals, smashing up the place just for fun. "How did I get *so* high?"

Zeus flopped over in his bed, flinging his arm across his face. "You took God's elevator," he mumbled.

She hid her face in her hands as the expected wave of remorse and embarrassment washed over her. If she hadn't gotten so fucked up, she might have been able to get a story. Instead, she'd lain zonked out on the floor, giggling with Nelson about the cartoon faces she saw in the wallpaper.

It doesn't matter. Marla already got the story they asked for, and who knows if they'd have bought another one.

Grace sighed and picked up her phone, stretched out on the bed, and opened her web browser. She went to *High Note's* webpage and found Marla's story already up. They didn't waste time editing gossip like this: if they didn't vomit it up quickly for everyone to see, someone else would.

Inez Carter has found a new love, or at least a new fling, the article read. Sources close to the singer reveal she's ended her relationship Mildred Easley, actress, accomplished socialite, and star of the hit drama Shaving Melissa. *Carter is now dating hot pants-enthusiast Nicole Watters, better known as BeatBot. The couple is said to have met at a recent cast party in Los Angeles. Is there a highly publicized gay wedding in their future? Only time will tell.*

And that was it, save for a couple paragraphs about stuff everyone already knew, such as Inez's very public stance on her sexuality and her role as an LGBTQ-rights activist.

Grace winced. That was really all that Lawrence had asked for: confirmation of the rumor he'd heard about Inez's new relationship. She should have called Lawrence as soon as Nelson had told her the rumor was true; she could have beaten Marla to the punch.

Where had Marla gotten her information, anyhow? Had she been able to talk to someone before she'd been kicked out? The only reliable source in the room had been Nelson. Grace's heart squeezed as she pictured the two of them flirting and talking. Had Grace been playing second fiddle to the other freelancer in that regard, as well?

Grace had thought Nelson liked her, but he'd probably just been a tool on the hunt for a toolbox, like any other guy. He hadn't cared enough to give her his number, or even say goodbye last night. She'd lost track of him when she'd become involved in an extended, late-night jam session involving accordions and penny whistles and a harpsichord—a *harpsichord*, what sort of weirdo rich fucks had one of those? When she'd emerged, Nelson was gone.

Grace heaved herself up and took a shower.

Lyssa Medlin's practice space was in an old office building that had been converted to artists' studios. The sound of multiple bands practicing thumped through the walls.

Muffled laughter and the sound of someone tuning a violin came from within Lyssa's room. Zeus went to knock, but Grace caught his wrist first and fixed him with a serious stare. "Remember what we talked about," she whispered. "Try to act, like, semi-normal. This is a huge opportunity."

Zeus gazed at her with his big eyes, then hung his head slightly and nodded. Grace released his wrist. *It's for his own good, she thought.* Zeus mostly didn't realize how weird he was, and Gracie hated the look of pain in his eyes when people's reaction to him was different than he expected.

He couldn't afford to learn the hard way. Not this time. This was big.

Zeus rapped on the door. It opened, and Lyssa Medlin smiled at them with her cute, crooked teeth. "Hey, it's the guitar genius! Come on in."

They stepped into a large, windowless room wallpapered in shag carpet and blacklight unicorn posters. A surprising number of other musicians were already there, fiddling with a wide collection of instruments. Zeus glanced around, gently cradling Grace's electric guitar—the one nonessential item she'd kept out of storage, on his behalf.

"Everyone, this is Zeus," Lyssa said, then turned to Grace. "And I'm sorry, I don't know your name."

"Grace."

"And Grace."

The other musicians gave waves or nods, and one guy with short hair and a chin-strap beard put down his bass and stepped forward to shake Zeus's hand. "I saw you play last night. That was freakin' incredible. Hanging from the chandelier like a boss."

"Thank you," Zeus said. "I was on acid."

There were snickers from around the room.

Lyssa grinned, tossed back her curly brown pigtails, and stepped behind her keyboard. "Let's get started. We're going to play you one of my new songs." She squinted at Zeus thoughtfully. "I have a couple lead guitar parts in mind, but why don't we just see what you can do."

Zeus plugged into the tube amp Lyssa indicated, and the band launched into a standard rock tune with a catchy melody. Zeus listened for a moment, then, in just the right spot, he added a wonky lick.

The rest of the band members exchanged surprised looks…which Zeus missed, since he was curled around his guitar, playing another perfect line: understated, unexpected, and yet undeniably just what the song needed.

Grace smiled to herself. *That's my boy.*

After practice, they all went out for sushi. All anyone could talk about was Zeus's guitar playing. "Where did you go to school?" Lyssa asked, her eyes shining "How did you learn to play like that?"

Zeus picked at the stitching on his menu, shooting shy glances at the frontwoman. "I went to Wallingford High in Seattle, but they moved me to alternative school because the teachers said I was disruptive to the learning process, so I only have my GED."

There was silence around the long table. "You didn't go to music school?" the drummer asked.

Zeus pressed his lips together and shook his head. School was a sore subject for him, Grace knew. He had loved it, but it hadn't loved him back.

The violinist grinned, her upturned nose wrinkling into a button. "I hate you," she said.

Grace had done her research this time. The violinist had gone to Juilliard, so she'd studied hard trying to approach the skill level that Zeus had reached through self-teaching.

Zeus's hurt look faded to a tentative smile as he realized Heidi was joking. "Don't hate, don't hate," he retorted.

Grace was sitting next to the bass player, Don, the one with the chinstrap beard who had been at the party. "So, are you, like, with that drummer from Karma Korn?" he asked, sucking down edamame.

Grace's shoulders hunched. "No. We're just friends, I guess. I only met him yesterday."

"Ah," Don said. He chewed thoughtfully. "I actually thought he was with Inez Carter for a while, because they are like *always* together, you know? And it was weird, because she's supposedly gay. I eventually figured out they just have this bizarre relationship. But…" He paused, quirking his fleshy lips. "You know, I don't think she's really gay. She's bisexual or something."

A waiter set plates of food in front of them. So, Don had also noticed it. "Yeah," Grace said. "What's up with that?"

Don shrugged and tucked a napkin into the collar of his Atari t-shirt. "Good question. It seems a strange thing to lie about, but people are weird."

"Especially in this business," Grace said, and they both snorted.

Lyssa raised her voice above the chatter of conversation. "So." Everyone quieted, and she glanced around the table at her gigantic-to-the-point-of-cultishness-band, finally resting her gaze on Zeus. "I'd usually have, like, some sort of band meeting about this, but I'm pretty sure I speak for all of us when I ask if you'll join the band, Zeus."

Zeus blinked. He had been curled up in a rare bout of self-consciousness, but he straightened his back and raised his hands in the air. "The cool kids on the playground asked me to play with them." He beamed. "Of course I'll play with you."

There was clapping all around. The violinist cheered, and Don reached past Grace to give Zeus a fist bump.

Under the table, Zeus reached over and squeezed Grace's hand. She could feel him vibrating like a high-tension wire, and she had a pang of anxiety, wondering how he'd deal with the pressure.

Maybe I can make a killing writing articles about his antics, she thought, nervously.

———

Back at the motel, Grace flopped on the bed while Zeus tried to burn off some of his energy with a manic bout of push-ups. She pulled out her laptop and started working on an article she'd been hired to write by *Keyboard Tech* magazine at twenty-five cents a word. Every time she finished typing a sentence, she imagined herself buying a soda with the proceeds.

Someday, I'll be rich enough to afford soda again, she thought.

Zeus started in on jumping jacks, singing a Bruno Mars song. Grace sighed and rubbed her temples.

Zeus stopped singing, but kept jumping. "What's wrong, Gracie? Why are you so sad?"

Grace quickly put her hands back on the keyboard. "Nothing. I'm fine."

"Don't bool-shit a bool-shit-er." He did a few thoughtful jumping jacks, then tittered. "Booo-ooowl-ooowl SHIT. I wonder if you could train cattle to knock down bowling pins with their poop? I mean, they'd have to get some force behind it, but maybe you could manage it with the right diet. Bullshit Bowling. But no, really, Gracie. What's wrong?"

She squeezed her sandy eyes shut, fighting back a wave of dull fatigue. "I just wonder why I bother with this stuff sometimes. I have this stupid dream of being able to make it as a freelancer so I have time for music and my own writing-"

"And for Bullshit Bowling with me."

"And for Bullshit Bowling with you, yes. But Mitch was right. My parents are right. It's a stupid dream. I should be looking for full-time jobs, not wasting my time with this crap. I'm being immature."

Zeus abandoned the jumping jacks and started in on squats. "Being immature is where it's at, though. Look how most adults are, with their scrunched-up, pissed-off faces. They want us to get off their lawns because they secretly wish they were out playing with us. They've got a bad taste in their souls because of how they've chosen to live."

"Well, they've *chosen* to live in a way that allows them to have a house, and food on the table, and the option of not dying destitute and alone. I'd say it's a pretty rational trade-off."

Zeus came to sit on the bed beside Grace. He ruffled her hair. "You'll never die alone, Gracie, because you have me. And you won't die destitute, either. Cheer up. We have this motel room, and we've got food. We have everything we need, actually."

"But for how long?" she moaned. "If I don't start making more money-"

"Shhh. Let tomorrow worry about itself. You're working hard, and you're doing the right thing. Forget about the super lame stuff everyone else wants, how everyone else thinks you should live. This is what you want to do, your dream. Right now that involves living in a motel and eating food from the dollar store. It might get better later, but this isn't so bad. Cups of noodles are good, and the maids clean up after us, and the smells in this place are interesting. Each one tells its own story."

"Thanks, Zeus." She hated herself for what she was about to say, but she had to say it. "You know, though, when you go off on tour or whatever with Lyssa Medlin, you'll take your SSI money with you. In fact, you'll probably lose it, because you'll be earning money. So I have to figure this stuff out pretty quick now, or I *will* be destitute." *And alone.*

Zeus stiffened, and Grace looked up to find him staring at his lap with a lost expression.

She snapped her mouth shut. She, in no way, ever wanted him to think she only kept him around for his money. But, since she'd lost her job, she'd relied on his checks to pay their expenses. She didn't know if she'd be able to make this freelancing experiment work without that cash, and that uncertainty nagged at her like an overly anxious grandmother. Did she have the right to gamble like that with his money?

She reached out and tentatively put her hand on his knee. "Zeus-"

He looked up at her sharply. "You won't come with me? If I do end up on tour?"

She blinked. "Huh?"

"You could still work at the freelancing stuff. You could even do a big article about us, and about the other bands. Someone would pay for that, Gracie. And you'd have time to write your own novel, too, and for music."

She sat there, not knowing what to say. It was a crazy idea, but it had its appeal. "You'd really want that? I'm like your mom or something. Why would you want me on tour with you?"

Zeus pounded the mattress, his eyes suddenly wild. "You're not my mom. My mom's a crack-brained and broken animal. You're my friend, Gracie. You're only nine and a half years older than me. And I want you around. I need you around."

She could see him trembling, and her heart hammered. She hadn't meant to set him off. He could get volatile when he got in these moods—running out and disappearing for days, refusing to eat…she had to be careful what she said. "Really?"

He rolled his eyes so hard that his whole head moved with them. "*Yes*, really." He stared at his knees, but his expression calmed, and Grace heaved an inward sigh of relief.

If Zeus went on tour without her, he'd be on his own for the first time since his mother abandoned him. Grace had been telling herself that he was ready to fly the coop, but she couldn't stop herself from picturing him climbing the scaffolding around the stage or running off after some shiny object and missing a show.

The band and the manager will take care of him, she thought. *He's really no worse than the one guy in the group that always drinks too much…* But was she willing to risk being wrong? Could she live with herself if he destroyed this chance at happiness—or worse—on tour?

Regardless, she couldn't deny that she *wanted* to go with him. Going wasn't the mature thing, and maybe not the right thing, but touring sounded like a blast.

She smiled tentatively. "Okay. I'd come with you."

His lips tightened. "You promise? You promise you'll stay with me?"

Grace frowned, taken aback by his vehemence. "Yeah, of course. I'll stay with you if that's really what you want."

The tension went out of his shoulders. He fidgeted with a frayed spot in the quilt. Then he stood and fished in his jeans pocket, pulling out a scrap of paper. He tossed it onto the bed next to her. "I forgot. Nelson gave me his number to give to you last night. He couldn't find you when he left."

Her stomach curdled, and she swallowed hard. "You *forgot?*"

He gazed back defiantly before turning on his heel and stalking off to the bathroom.

Grace ran the scrap of paper between her fingers. The realization hit her like a bad bout of flu: Zeus had played her almost as adeptly as he played guitar. She'd been so worried about him that she hadn't thought what she might be giving up by promising to stay with him.

Her thoughts churned. She loved Zeus. To her, he was half son, half best friend. But was this relationship healthy? Did he really still need her, or did they cling to one another out of habit and desperation? Would they end up dragging each other down?

This relationship has gotten way weird.

It didn't matter now, she realized. She'd promised to stay with him, and she wouldn't renege. He'd been abandoned and lied to enough in his life. Maybe he'd been manipulative in holding back Nelson's number, but could she blame him for having issues?

She'd find a way to stay with him as long as he wanted her around, and to make a living meanwhile. If any man she might be interested in (she tried hard to not think of Nelson) didn't accept that Zeus was part of her life, well, he couldn't be the man for her.

But she wouldn't let Zeus take over her life and call all the shots. She scooped up her laptop and opened a new document.

As she composed the opening to a new article, she smiled grimly to herself. *I'll go on tour with him, but I'm no groupie. If he's gonna play, I'm gonna play, too.*

8

Grace waited, twisting the stem of her wineglass between her fingers. There were candles on the tables, vases of real orchids, and more silverware than was strictly necessary. This was a *date*. She hadn't been on a date since… she couldn't even remember, but practically since when a "date" involved hiding in the garage and getting drunk on illegally acquired beer. She wiped a droplet of sweat from her upper lip.

It hadn't been easy, calling Nelson. She'd forgotten the feeling of wondering how soon to call, what to say. Of second-guessing herself and the whole situation. In the end, she'd only hesitated for about five minutes after she'd finished writing her article before she'd picked up the phone.

Writing the piece hadn't taken her long, and she'd sent an email pitching it to Lawrence before her conscience could convince her not to. She reminded herself now that it had been the right thing to do. No matter how bumbling and inept she was at it, she was supposedly a journalist, and she couldn't be faulted for trying to turn everything into a story…even if she ran the risk of annoying people she cared about.

Especially when they deserve it.

The waiter came to refill her water for the third time. "Another glass of wine while you're waiting?" His slightly cocked eyebrow and gentle tone made her check her phone and realize she'd been waiting twenty-five minutes.

"Uh, sure," she said. "Another glass of wine. Why not."

She could see the pity in the waiter's courteous nod before he bustled off behind the bar, and she fought back a wave of anger and embarrassment. Why the fuck would Nelson ask her out on a date, then ditch her? Did all L.A. rock stars act like cruel junior high kids? Maybe he was live-tweeting the joke to his legions of followers right now. *Asked out some freaky acid-tripping journalist with grape slushie in her hair, and she actually took me seriously.*

Grace downed the last of her wine and glanced over at the bar, checking the progress of her next one. If Nelson didn't show, she'd just stay and get drunk by herself, even though it would eat up the last of her meager credit.

Just as her wine arrived and she was about to give free rein to her self-pity, Nelson came through the door with a harried look. He plopped down in the chair opposite her. He sighed heavily and ran his fingers through his bushy, red hair.

"I'm *so* sorry I'm late."

Relief and happiness brought a smile to Grace's face, but she managed to salvage a scowl out of the situation. "Yeah, I'll say. I was about to go flash my boobs on the corner to try to lure in a replacement date."

He snorted. "In this neighborhood, you would've just attracted a swarm of film school graduates asking you to star in a short piece about urban angst."

Grace's heart softened at the look of pure misery on his face. "What's up? What happened?"

He tugged at his beard, avoiding her eyes. "Inez wouldn't let me leave. You know how bandmates can be, especially when it's their project. She gets obsessive about getting things right sometimes." He smiled. "Anyway, I'm sorry. Will you forgive me?"

Grace squinted across the table, trying to picture a woman who cut a recording session short to be with the man who threw a chow mein noodle at a sound engineer as a woman "obsessive about getting things right." Grace didn't blame Nelson for not telling the truth, though: she was a journalist, after all, and he was probably worried she'd write an article about whatever stupid stunt Inez Carter had pulled to cause the delay.

Grace suffered a new twinge of guilt. She hadn't even thought about how much it might piss off *Nelson* if the piece she had just sent Lawrence got published. *But it serves him right, too. He gave info to Marla before I showed up. Besides, it's not like he didn't know I was after a story.*

If this ever grew into a relationship (she shuddered just slightly), she and Nelson would have to learn to trust one another. But for now, it was just a date, and he seemed like a good enough guy.

And he was good-looking. And he smelled nice.

She smiled. "I forgive you."

Nelson ordered a Belgian craft beer, and Grace, awash in nerves, chugged down her fresh glass of wine and ordered another. Soon she found herself giggling over appetizers: "If it's so anti-pasta, I'd better not order the linguini. We don't want there to be a smackdown on the table."

Nelson mimed punches. "Pow, pow! Take that, you lousy noodle-head."

Knowing she had to drive, Grace cut herself off, only three glasses too late. By the time her herb and pancetta-crusted chicken arrived, she was expounding on rave culture. "It was a lot different when we were in college. Back then, it'd be a group of more ambitious musical friends renting out a warehouse and throwing this huge tripped-out underground drug party, trying not to attract the attention of the police. Now, shit, LiveNation is in on the deal."

Nelson nodded. "They smelled all the money kids will beg off their parents to go to these things."

Grace giggled. "I still think raves are fun, though. Gen X ravers will be throwing raves in our nursing homes." She took a too-large sip of her wine. "Maybe we should throw a geriatric-themed rave now."

Nelson laughed. "I can imagine all the people dancing with walkers, their pants pulled up to their armpits."

"The DJ dropping Duke Ellington and Barry Manilow samples…chicks dancing in cages, fully clothed in flower-print, lace-collared dresses, throwing Ben Gay-flavored condoms to the crowd…"

Nelson winced and shook his head, snickering, and Grace hoped she hadn't gone too far. *Ben Gay-flavored condoms? Gross.* Jesus, she shouldn't drink.

She quickly segued into a somewhat less tasteless—or bad-tasting—subject. "Speaking of raves…" She rubbed her nose while staring down at her chicken. "I'm really sorry I got so high the other night."

He laughed. "It wasn't even your fault. And you were super cute, to tell you the truth. I'd do acid with you any day."

Warmth spread through her, and she lifted her gaze to his. "Thanks."

"And Zeus hanging from the chandelier…" Nelson rocked with silent laughter, his blue eye sparkling. "That was one of the best things I've ever seen."

Grace hid a smile behind her hand. "Did you know Lyssa Medlin asked him to play in her band because of it?"

"Seriously? No, I didn't know. That's awesome!"

"I know, right?"

"That's LA at its best," Nelson said. "Getting a gig because you got high on acid and caused a ruckus."

"Yeah." Grace fidgeted with her napkin. She told herself she was only going to ask because she was curious, that it had nothing to do with an article. "And you know, Inez tackling him afterward…it seems like she really has a crush on him."

Nelson's shoulders sagged a bit and the sparkle left his eyes. "Yeah. I mean, I don't know if she really likes him like that, or if she's just being Inez. I love her to death, but she's kind of a player."

Grace snorted into her wine. "Poor Nicole." *And poor Zeus.* Zeus was tough enough to deal with women like Inez. *Right?* If he wasn't, Grace would deal with women like Inez herself.

Nelson grimaced. "Poor everyone she dates. I guess I understand why Duke tries to get her to project an image of someone with a more stable love life. But, I hate to say it, I think the hot mess rock star thing is working for her… career-wise, I mean. Duke really thinks otherwise. His assistant told him to leave Inez be, to not try to meddle, and Duke got so mad at him the assistant quit."

Grace's eyebrows shot up. "Tristan? The creepy guy?"

Nelson smirked. "That's the one. It was a huge kerfuffle."

That must have been what their little whispered conversation had been at the rave, after Inez had tackled Zeus. Grace shook her head, marveling again at the strangeness of her adopted town.

Grace spent the ill-advised drive back to the motel rolling every scene of the date through her head, subjecting it to careful dissection. Nelson was easy to talk to, and funny. Had she dominated the conversation, though? And had she been funny enough, or had the wine just made her *think* she was funny?

But he *had* asked her on another date, to see one of his friend's bands play at a club in Hollywood that Friday. And he'd kissed her when they'd said goodbye. She could still feel the pressure of his lips on hers, and how his beard had tickled her face.

She pulled herself out of the reverie just in time to keep herself from running a red light.

When she opened the motel room door, she found Zeus standing on the little desk, peering intently at the fire sprinkler embedded in the popcorn ceiling.

"How did your date go?" he asked, without looking at her.

She eyed the sagging top of the cheap desk nervously. "Pretty good." She put her purse down and leaned against the wall. "How's your date with the sprinkler going?"

His expression grew even stonier. "I'm just wondering if they could gas us with this thing."

"The answer to that is no, Zeus."

He turned to fix her with an intense gaze. "Just because you believe something is true doesn't make it true. What if they had gassed me when you were gone, and you'd come back to find my twisted, blue corpse wadded up in the corner?"

"That would have been super shitty."

"Would you have cried?"

"Of course. A lot. It would have been the worst thing that could ever happen to me."

He frowned and muttered something she couldn't hear.

Grace hugged herself. "Zeus, come down from there. They're not going to gas us, I promise. Bala is a good guy, and he's not going to murder his paying guests. It'd fuck up his profit margin."

"I think we should tape something over it, just to be sure. Like a sock, or no, one of the pillows would be better."

"We can't do that. Bala would have a fit." She held out her hand. "Come down. Please?"

He regarded her hand warily and jumped down without touching it. He went to stand in the corner, where he stared at the wall with hunched shoulders.

Grace sighed. "Zeus, please don't be mad at me."

"I'm not mad."

"So this is totally cool behavior then?"

He glanced at her, his eyes angry. He looked like he was about to say something, but Grace's phone began to vibrate in her purse, and he didn't.

Her heart raced as she dug through old lipsticks and dirty plastic cutlery, looking for it. Was it Nelson calling? Had he remembered her Ben Gay comment and decided to cancel their date?

She found it and checked the screen. It was Lawrence. Adrenaline surged through her, and she punched the answer icon. "Hello?"

"Hey, Grace," he said. "Sorry for calling so late."

"That's okay." Zeus was staring at her, and her grip tightened on the phone. "You read the article, then?"

"I sure did."

She sat down on the bed with her back toward Zeus. "And?"

"This is quite the story. Are you sure about your sources?"

"Absolutely. It's based on first-hand observation." She'd decided not to tell Lawrence that the main subject of the article was in the room with her now. It would seem cheesy.

"Seriously?" Lawrence said.

"Yep. I've been doing some Gonzo Reporting." There was another silence, and Grace realized with disgust that Lawrence had probably never heard of Hunter S. Thompson, probably didn't know what Gonzo Reporting was. "I'm an embedded reporter, you might say. It's a unique opportunity, and you might be able to reap some benefits from it."

"Totally," he said. "We're definitely interested in this story, and perhaps others from your insider perspective."

Grace was momentarily dizzy with relief and happiness. She'd be able to buy a whole *case* of soda with this money if she was smart about it. "You want the article, then? How about two dollars a word?"

His tone dried up like a slug in the sun. "The senior editors thought the story was pretty good, but there's no way they'd do two dollars a word. They were thinking more like seventy-five cents."

Grace blew a raspberry, then realized that was the wine talking. She cleared her throat. "I'll bet *Celebrity Life* would buy this one, and they'd pay me way more than seventy-five cents."

They haggled a bit, and Grace realized Lawrence was more interested in the article than he was letting on. By the time they came to an agreement, she had talked him into a buck-fifty a word. Since the article was around three thousand words, she'd just made more money in a few hours of work than she'd made in the last two months of hustling as a low-level freelancer.

Lawrence had the balls to end their negotiations with another invitation to drinks. "To celebrate your success," he said.

Grace winced. "I'd love to, but I have a few more articles to get in for other magazines," she half-lied. "I'll call you when things slow down a bit." He agreed, with a petulant note in his voice, and she hung up quickly.

Grace let out a whoop, feeling lighter than she had in ages.

Zeus spoke in a flat tone. "You sold an article?"

Her victorious laughter died on her lips, and she clutched her knees. "Yeah."

"That's cool. What was the article about?"

She faced him hesitantly. His arms were crossed, and he wasn't smiling; it suddenly struck her what a formidable figure he cut, with his six-foot-three, hundred-and-seventy pounds of too-many-pushups muscle. But she could also see the scared and hurt little boy in him, and that was what worried her more.

"Zeus…" All the breath went out of her, and she hid her face in her hands. Just at the moment, her reasons for writing the article without discussing it with him seemed petty and childish. He may have pissed her off, but two wrongs didn't make a right. She was supposed to be the adult here.

Though that was a joke if she'd ever heard one. She had him living in a motel and going to acid parties. Courtney Love would make a better foster parent.

"What did you do, Gracie? Did you write about Inez and me? Are you going to get Inez in trouble for not being gay?"

Grace took her hands from her face, her brow furrowing. "That's a weird way of putting it. 'In trouble for not being gay.'"

"But it's true. You know how people are, jealous of how their group's identity is perceived. She'll get mobbed and flim-flammed like you wouldn't believe, if that's what the article was about."

Grace tugged at her lip. "Well, but if she's bisexual, she should just say so." Though, to be honest, Grace knew firsthand that the lesbian community could be just as harsh to bisexuals as straight people were. There was this one lesbian she'd had a fling with in college…Grace shook her head to clear it. Is that why Inez was lying about her sexuality? To avoid anti-bi sentiment?

Grace sighed. "No matter what her orientation is, she shouldn't spend all that time man-bashing, if you ask me."

Zeus scoffed. "Men can take a bit of bashing if we're anywhere near as manly as we say we are. Goodness knows men do enough bashing themselves." His eyes became focused in his elsewhere. "Bash! Bash bash! What a weird word. Bash! Bash bong bing! Puh-pow pow pow pow pow. Tink. Bash!" He giggled to himself and muttered something about ghosts.

The real world slowly drew him back, his gaze finding her again. "So, *is* that what the article is about? Me and Inez being, like, semi-in-love or something?"

She rubbed her nose with her fist, looking anywhere but at him. "Well, sorta."

"What sorta, Gracie? Sorta what? Sorta this, that, or the other? What kind of sorta?"

She made herself meet his eyes. "The article actually centers on *you*. About you busting into the studio and meeting Inez. About you hanging from the chandelier and playing guitar, and about how Lyssa asked you to be in her band."

She tensed as she watched this information sink in, waiting for him to slam the door as he stalked out, or jump back up on the desk and start tearing out the fire sprinkler, or lock himself in the bathroom and destroy all her makeup by making an angry collage. Instead, he blinked, and a smile grew on his face. "About *me*? But why would they want to publish an article about *me*?"

Her mouth opened, closed again, opened, and she couldn't stop a relieved giggle from escaping. "Because it's an interesting story, with lots of inside celebrity gossip. I portray you as the amazingly talented new kid on the scene." She examined his face closely, her shoulders relaxing somewhat. "You're really not mad at me?"

He jumped up on his bed and started bouncing; the long-suffering springs groaned in protest. "No way! That's awesome! I'm gonna be in a magazine!"

She grinned. "Yep. And they're paying me a lot of money. We'll be able to pay a deposit on an apartment, if I can convince the manager I have a steady source of income."

Zeus jumped across the gap onto Grace's bed, then flopped down beside her, pulling her into a breath-stealing hug. "Yay. An apartment. We'll have a home again."

Grace laughed. "Sure will." She leaned her forehead on his shoulder, feeling lighter in her soul. At least Zeus wasn't mad at her. If Nelson got miffed at the way she'd portrayed Inez, well, that was too bad. At this point, earning enough money for them to have a stable home was more important than keeping her friends. *And besides, telling the truth is supposedly what journalism is all about.*

As she chanted this mantra, trying to keep her guilt at bay, she wondered if perhaps she didn't have the best temperament to be a celebrity gossip reporter, or even a resident of Los Angeles.

9

Grace's article got edited down to 2,500 words, but *High Note* put it on the homepage of their website, which more than made up for the cuts. It was a different sort of article than those mags usually ran, an in-depth narrative focusing on a complete unknown, but the other players were big enough and the story was compelling enough that Grace had hopes it would get her noticed.

It was Friday morning when it went up, and Grace and Zeus sat side-by-side on her bed, reading it on her laptop.

Zeus giggled and pointed at the screen. "'…*good-looking and talented enough to make Inez Carter consider switching sides.*' I want a t-shirt that says that. But I don't think she's switching sides, because sexuality isn't like a civil war or trading football players, Gracie."

"Touché. But how do you explain her sudden turnabout from being a lesbian to liking a dude?"

Zeus shrugged. "Maybe she's discovering new things about herself. Or maybe I'm just so awesome even lesbians are attracted to me. Or maybe she's just been infected with the virus of straight propaganda."

Grace snorted. "All those things are possible, I suppose. Have you heard from Inez, by the way? You gave her your number, right?"

Zeus nodded, then shook his head. "I gave her my number and the motel phone but she hasn't called. Not a peep. Not a squeak or squawk or honk, nor any of the less popular animal noises."

Grace squinted at him. "I thought she would have. She seemed to really be into you."

Zeus shrugged and bounced off the bed onto his feet. "Come on. You're driving me to practice, right? You should stay this time. Maybe someone will do something noteworthy, like get pregnant, or get amnesia. Maybe someone's evil twin will show up."

Grace flipped her laptop closed. "Okay, I'm coming."
**

Grace sat on the sofa in the practice room while the band played, her fingers itching to play an instrument along with them. She was digging hearing the songs come together. About an hour in, though, things became uncomfortable.

The band was in the middle of working through a new piece when the horn player blew a foul note, the vibraphone player screwed up an arpeggio, and the drummer somehow lost a stick, which catapulted into the ride cymbal with a loud *pang*.

Lyssa raised her eyebrows, smirking, and Zeus coaxed a

complicated ker-plink-plank out of his guitar that sounded like a jalopy crashing into a bucket of bolts, grinding the song to a messy halt.

"Boosh!" Zeus said. "Everyone alright? No fatalities in that wreck?"

The drummer laughed. "Sorry," she said, wincing.

"It wasn't just you," the vibe player said. "Some sort of catastrophe happened."

The horn player, a lanky young woman named Drea, wrinkled her nose and mimed throwing her French horn across the room. "I can't play this fucking thing, Lyssa. I mean, seriously. I'm a trumpet player."

The vibraphone player shrugged, lightly tapping the keys with his mallets, practicing the part he'd flubbed. "I don't know how to play this thing, either. I'm a keyboard player. I just give it the best whack I can." He whacked the keys. *Plonk*.

"Yeah, but at least the notes are the same on the vibraphone as on your piano," Drea huffed. "This horn is way different than the trumpet. You key it differently and you have to blow in a completely different way. How are we supposed to learn a new song if we have to learn new instruments, too?"

A shuffling silence ensued, the rest of the band avoiding looking at Drea; all except Zeus, who was watching her as if she were a fascinating documentary.

Lyssa gazed out at her small army of a band, tapping

her thumb against the hollow body of her guitar. "Do you really feel you can't play the part on the French horn, Drea?"

Drea tossed back her curtain of silvery hair. "I think it's ridiculous that you're expecting us to play all these different instruments. I signed on as a trumpet player, period. I feel like if I'm going to have to play French horn or trombone or auto harp or whatever the fuck you'll have me playing next, I should get paid more, because of how much of my free time I have to spend practicing."

Quite a few band members adopted expressions that suggested they were late for dentist appointments.

The vibe player frowned. "We all spend free time practicing, Drea, even if it's just on our regular instruments. That's what being a musician is about. Playing new instruments is a great opportunity to expand our musical knowledge. Just think of it that way."

"Any issues of pay can be brought up at band meeting," Lyssa said. "Now isn't the right time to discuss it. But everyone agreed on the payment schedule, and I think it was quite fair. If this is just about money…"

Drea's shoulders hunched. "No, it's not really about the money," she said, her tone milder. "I just don't want to go out in front of God and everyone sounding like total crap."

The atmosphere in the room lightened a little. Fighting about money issues at practice was something only the most sadistic of musicians relished. "Well," Lyssa said. "If you're having trouble playing the part, that's a separate issue. I mean, you could just play it on the trumpet instead…"

The bass player, groaned. "Noooooo. It sounds so much better on the French horn. It'd be too in-your-face brassy on the trumpet."

Drea and several others' mouths opened to lodge an opinion, but they stopped when Zeus shyly raised his hand, looking around at all of them with wide, golden eyes. Lyssa smiled. "Yes, Zeus?"

His hand fell back to his guitar and he fiddled with the strings. "I just wanted to say that your French horn part is sounding great, Drea. I think the song is coming together really well. Part of the problem could be that we're all worried about sounding too slick and professional, like we're playing at some rich doofus's wedding and the bride will beat us to death with her bouquet if we play a single wrong note. But a huge part of the beauty of music comes from a certain amount of wrong-footedness. I mean, look at Thelonious Monk; he sounded like he was watching a baseball game and forgot he was playing a song half the time. And he's one of the granddaddies of music."

There were nods around the room. Some of the petulance left Drea's face, and she looked thoughtful.

"I think all this instrument-switching is really cool," Zeus continued, "and it's a great opportunity to add magic to the music. A little bit of the unexpected, of beautiful imperfection. It allows people to relate to the music more, because they can see the humanity behind it."

The bass player grinned and clapped. "Yeah!"

"Well said," the drummer added. "I agree completely."

Grace gave Zeus a surreptitious thumbs-up as a hesitant smile grew on Drea's face.

"I get what you're saying," Drea said. "I just don't want to sound *too* wrong-footed…"

"You're sounding great, you really are," Lyssa said. "And I agree with Zeus, too. I think a bit of edginess could sound really awesome, like the horn parts in Neutral Milk Hotel's *Aeroplane Over the Sea*. Or maybe even edgier than that. Thelonious Monk style, like Zeus said."

Drea nodded again. "Okay, I'll give it another try."

There was a rustling as the band members readied themselves to resume playing. Lyssa smiled wide at Zeus, her eyes shining, then reached up to gently tweak his nose.

"Thanks Zeus," she muttered, quiet enough that only Zeus and Grace, who was sitting nearest them, could hear.

A tinge of color rose to Zeus' cheeks as he smiled back at the band leader. Then Lyssa squared her shoulders and spun the volume knob on her guitar. "From the beginning again. One, two, three, one, two, three."

The band launched back into the song. Grace watched Lyssa closely, noticing that the frontwoman's eyes slid over to watch Zeus a lot more frequently than necessary, as if she were singing just to him.

**

Zeus sang Lyssa's songs all the way home, pounding his thighs to the beat and screeching out his guitar solos. When he started warbling a little too loudly and flailing his head around, Grace cleared her throat.

"So," she said. "Good practice, huh?"

"Yeah, it was really cool. Deedle-duh-dee pink pink-"

"I was wondering how Lyssa kept a band that big together. With all those personalities, it has to be a nightmare. But she does a good job of wrangling them. And she seemed to be really happy about how you helped her calm Drea down today."

"I didn't really help. Buh-WAH-duddle-bing! I was just expressing my opinion, and Drea was cool, she was just having herself a moment. Krankety-zipeeee—"

Grace smirked, studying him from the corner of her eye. "I think you're integrating really well into the band. And Lyssa is pretty into you, huh?"

"Yeah, she seems to like me. Beedle-bow, puh-planky bow bow. I rock the guitar pretty well, right? I stick my licks in all the places she likes. Oh, my God, that sounds nasty. Buh-bow-bow-squeeeeeeee-"

"Yeah, but that's my point, Zeus." Grace gave him a meaningful look as they rolled to a stop in traffic.

Zeus quit squinky-ginking and gazed at her a moment, his mouth sliding into an "o". "Nuh uh. She doesn't like me that sticky-inny-nasty way."

Grace snickered. "Does too. I'm an expert at these things."

He fell silent, gazing out the windshield, his dexterous fingers tapping out guitar licks on his thigh. "That's crazy," he muttered.

Grace hid her grin behind her fist. "Yeah, well. The heart wants what it wants."

His brow creased. "But she likes my guitar playing, too, right?"

"Of course. How could she not?"

His brow smoothed. "Okay, that's cool then. As long as I'm not just some hired dick." He started warbling again.

Grace's smile faded and she chewed her lip. As cute as it was that Lyssa had a crush on Zeus, Grace hoped the songwriter was mature and professional enough to keep it under wraps. Those sorts of dynamics could kill a band quicker than a bad batch of heroin.

**

Grace spent the afternoon looking at some-day-soon-maybe apartments online and working on another boring tech article. Zeus watched the Discovery Channel and played the guitar, unplugged. Grace was about to get up to start primping for her second date with Nelson— an early dinner followed by his friend's show—when her phone rang.

She had an attack of jitters when she saw it was Nelson calling. She pushed the answer icon. "Hello?"

"Hey, Grace."

Her stomach hollowed. He sounded like a man with bad news. "What's up?"

"Listen, something has come up…I'm not gonna be able to make it tonight."

A lump rose in her throat before she could stop it. "Oh. I'm really sorry. Is everything, you know, all right?"

There was a pause. Grace held her breath, wondering which she was about to get: a transparent excuse or a lie. When he spoke, she could tell it was neither.

"Inez is in the hospital."

"Ohmygod." Her hand flew to her mouth. Zeus stopped playing and looked over at her. "Is she okay?" Grace asked. "What happened?"

There was another pause, longer this time, and Grace clutched a hand in her hair. She might regret this, but… "You can tell me, Nelson. I won't put it in an article. I'm taking my journalist hat off now."

He sighed. "It was apparently an overdose. Heroin they think."

Grace exchanged a look with Zeus, who came over and pressed his ear to the other side of the phone. "Oh, fuck, Nelson," Grace said. "I'm so sorry. They got to her in time, though, right?"

"Yeah, thank God. She wasn't breathing, but they brought her back."

Zeus' face fell to an uncharacteristic degree. "Oh crap," Grace muttered.

"I'm the one who found her. I wasn't even going to check on her tonight. I'm so glad I did."

"Me, too," Grace said. "So, so glad. Jesus. Are you at the hospital? I'd like to come see her. Not as a journalist, but, you know, as a friend."

There was no pause this time, and Grace was relieved. "I'd like that. I'm trying to keep this quiet, so I'm here alone, and I could use some company. And can you bring Zeus with you, too? She likes him, and it might help her to see him when she wakes up."

Zeus smiled, blushing faintly. Warmth spread through Grace, that Nelson would think to include Zeus. People so often left him out, and not because he was forgettable.

Grace put a hand on Zeus' shoulder. "Which hospital are you at? We'll be there in a jif."

**

Zeus frowned as they wove through traffic on the way to the hospital. "Heroin. That just doesn't fit. It's almost like a piece from a different puzzle. I mean, Inez is all manner of blitzed, but not on that stuff."

"Sometimes it's hard to tell," Grace said. In her heart, though, she agreed. There was a certain bleak aura heroin tended to give people, and Inez didn't have it. Maybe she had wanted to try some for the first time and had overdone it.

"You can't get hepatitis C from kissing someone, can you?" Zeus squirmed. "I mean, even if they're really sloppy about it?"

Grace glanced sidelong at him. "No, Zeus. You're gonna be okay."

His shoulders relaxed, though he muttered something about eating hand sanitizer.

Inez was in a private room at Cedars Sinai. They were known for their discretion in these matters, but Grace knew word of this would get out, and she cursed herself for promising not to be the one to leak it. An inside article on something like this would crack her career wide open.

Nelson sat at the singer's bedside, his face gray and pinched with worry. He stood when Grace and Zeus came in, and his expression seemed to brighten as his eyes met hers. *Or maybe I'm imagining it.*

He attempted a smile. "Hey. Thanks for coming."

Grace gave him a hug, all the unease about not breaking this story leaving her. Some things *were* more important than her job, though that attitude was probably the biggest thing holding her career back.

"How are you doing?" Grace asked.

Nelson sighed and relaxed his hold on her. "I'm doing okay, I guess."

Zeus gazed down at Inez's pale form huddled under the sheets. She looked like a discarded marionette, wired up with tubes and hospital paraphernalia. Her face was sunken, older than her twenty-two years; even her hair seemed duller than usual. Zeus gently took one of her hands, careful not to disturb the IV, but Inez didn't stir.

"So what happened?" Grace asked. "You found her in her hotel room?"

Nelson nodded. "We had a short day at the studio because of some software issues. I didn't really need to see her, but I decided I wanted to talk to her about one of the tracks. I just…I guess I had a feeling or something. I know it sounds silly."

Grace shook her head. "It doesn't. And it saved her life, so it can't be silly."

"I don't even want to think about what would have happened if I hadn't."

Zeus tenderly arranged Inez's hair about her face.

"I didn't know she did heroin," Grace said. "Zeus and I were talking about it, she just doesn't seem the type."

Nelson tugged at his beard. "Yeah, you know what, I didn't know either. And you're right, she isn't the type. Don't get me wrong, she's definitely a piece of work in some ways. I mean…" He rolled his eyes. "To tell you the truth, the real reason I was late to our date the other day is…*please* don't print this…"

"It's okay, Nelson," she said quickly. "I won't."

He looked relieved. "I was late because she took some weird drugs I don't even know the names of, and started to believe she had the power to manipulate electricity. She was sucking on the power cord to one of the tube amps. I had to call Nicole to babysit her."

Grace had to press her fist to her lips so she wouldn't laugh. Nelson gazed at her apologetically, and she shrugged. "It's okay, Nelson, I understand. I'm really flattered that you made it to our date at all under the circumstances."

Nelson smiled faintly. "All that aside, those hard drugs have never been her thing. When I walked in and found her..." He winced and ran a hand over his face. "She was all sprawled out, half on the couch, and she wasn't breathing. My first thought wasn't even drugs. I thought she'd been murdered. But there was no blood, and there was a needle beside her."

Grace put her arm around his waist and squeezed him. "It's going to be all right now. You got her here in time."

"I hope so." He gave Grace a shy glance, then slid his arm around her waist as well. Worry was etched into every line of his features, and she got a rush of compassion.

"It's nice of you to take care of her," Grace said.

He half nodded, half shrugged. "She was my best friend's little sister. He asked me to look after her before he died of leukemia, and I promised I would."

Grace blinked. "Whoa. Jeez."

"Yeah, sorry to, you know, get so heavy."

"No, that's…jeez."

Nelson gazed distantly at Inez. "She always wanted to be a rock star. I think she got the idea from me and her brother, since we were in a band together. So I'm doubly responsible for this mess. If she hadn't been pulled into this stupid lifestyle…"

"What? No way, Nelson. You're not responsible for anything besides saving her life, and doing an excellent job keeping your promise."

He grinned weakly. "Well, it turned into a good-paying job, too."

Grace laughed. She liked the feeling of his arm around her.

Inez stirred. Her eyelids cracked open, and she winced and twitched.

Zeus broke into a grin and squeezed her hand. "Welcome back."

Nelson took his arm from around Grace and went to Inez's bedside. He took Inez's other hand. "You okay?"

Inez winced harder. "Where the fuck am I?"

"The hospital," Nelson said. "You overdosed."

Her brow wrinkled faintly. "Overdosed?"

Nelson scowled. "Goddammit, Inez. Why the hell are you doing heroin?"

Inez squinted at him. "Heroin?"

Nelson shook his head in disgust.

"Heroin is bad for you," Zeus said, fussing with her sheets. "It's worse than Twinkies, Inez. Worse probably even than flying on Indonesian Airlines. You shouldn't do it."

Inez seemed to notice him for the first time and broke into a dazed grin. "Oh, hey. It's you."

She reached out, her skinny arm trailing IV lines, and weakly ruffled his hair. Her grin faded to a confused look again. "I didn't do any heroin. That's stupid. I don't know what you guys are talking about. Is this some sort of prank?

Is it my birthday or something?"

Zeus giggled. "That would be the best prank! Gracie, will you knock me out and put me in the hospital for my birthday? Please?"

Grace gave him The Look.

Nelson frowned, looking uncertain. "You really don't remember doing any heroin? They found a shit-ton of it in your bloodstream."

"Naw, I would never do that. It makes me all sleepy and pukey."

"You've done it before, then?" he asked.

She shrugged. "It was something to do. But that doesn't mean I'm gonna, like, go all Cobain on the shit. I definitely didn't do any lately, and I definitely didn't overdose."

"What's the last thing you remember?" Nelson asked.

She twisted her bottom lip between her fingers, her eyes hazing over. "It's weird, I don't remember all that well. I know I was on Twitter arguing with some cunt who said I was exploiting gay culture. She'd read some article that said I was straight, and said she knew where I was and was coming to find me."

Grace's stomach crumpled like an empty beer can in a drunk man's fist. Zeus broke into a grin. Grace widened her eyes and shook her head slightly at him, but he plowed ahead regardless.

"That was Gracie's article, I'll bet. She told everyone how you're gay for me, Inez."

There was a silence. Nelson turned suddenly wary eyes on Grace. "Article?"

She managed to hold his gaze. "The article was actually about Zeus, but I may have mentioned the, uh, friendship he and Inez have formed."

The temperature in the room dropped about thirty degrees. Zeus shuffled his feet, realizing his faux pas.

Grace withstood Nelson's glare defiantly. "I was just telling the truth. What's so wrong with that?"

"You put her in danger!"

She couldn't keep herself from flinching, or from feeling a pang of hurt at his anger. But she stood her ground. "That was never my intention. Besides, we don't know what happened. How would somebody make her overdose on heroin, anyway?"

Inez gazed dreamily between Grace and Nelson, then took Zeus's hand. "Don't worry about it, Nels. Gracie, could you do an article about how Zeus is so awesome, he's an honorary chick or something? That would explain everything. Then maybe everyone would calm down and stop trying to kill me with H bombs."

Grace opened her mouth, then closed it again, not sure of the correct response to this. Nelson tore his eyes from hers and looked back at Inez. "What else do you remember?"

Inez frowned. "I…God, this is so weird. I vaguely remember opening the door for someone, but then everything just goes blank."

"You don't remember what the person looked like, who you opened the door for?" Nelson asked.

Inez shook her head. "No. I just remember someone knocking and getting up to answer it. I could have dreamed it, I guess."

Grace chewed her lip as she tried to put that together. How *would* someone have gotten Inez to overdose without her even knowing she was taking drugs? Especially a complete stranger from the internet? It didn't make sense, but Inez wasn't known for her normal, stable behavior. Maybe taking candy from strangers was par for the course for her. Or maybe she was just flat-out lying.

The burn of Nelson's glare soon pulled Grace back to reality, and her eyes fell to her feet. "I'm sorry," she muttered. "I really am. I'll just go."

She was hoping Nelson would protest, but he didn't say anything. Grace raised her eyebrows weakly at Zeus.

Zeus squeezed Inez's hand, then frowned at Nelson. "I guess we gotta go. I guess some people don't understand journalism, and telling the truth, and needing to make a living so that they can feel proud of themselves and not have to eat so many microwave burritos. I guess some people don't understand the difference between correlation and causation, either. Come on, Gracie."

Zeus shot Nelson an imperious look as they went out.

As soon as they were in the hallway, Grace put her arm around Zeus and gave him a squeeze. "Thanks, Zeus."

He stopped to slather his hands in sanitizer from a dispenser before hugging her back. "We don't need those germy chumps anyway, Gracie. We've got each other. And our careers." They smiled at one another.

"I'm glad," Grace said.

He jerked his chin toward the dispenser. "Let's decontaminate ourselves of this situation."

She nodded and squirted some goo on her hands, rubbing them together vigorously. "You were apparently right, you know. What you said about my article stirring up shit."

"But you were right too, Gracie. You have to tell the truth. You couldn't have foreseen that someone might get all homicidal-ish about it, if that's what even happened. And the truth about Inez not being purebred lesbian would have come out eventually anyway."

"I guess you're right."

But the anger in Nelson's eyes had hurt more than Grace wanted to admit.

As they turned the corner in the hallway, they almost ran into a slim, stiff-walking man dressed all in black. All three of them stopped short. "Oh!" Grace said. It was Duke's former assistant, Tristan.

"That was a close call," Zeus said, shifting on his feet beneath the man's stony glare. "I think we're all lucky to be alive, actually."

The assistant dusted off his immaculately black button-down shirt and slacks as if the near collision had sullied them. Grace, overcome by a nervousness she couldn't place, stepped aside for him to pass. He made no move to do so but stood examining her with impassive brown eyes. "You're the gossip mag journalist." His voice was younger and higher pitched than she had expected, but still quietly imposing.

Grace drew herself up. "I'm a freelance journalist."

Tristan's stony expression didn't change, but he still seemed to be sneering. "Really great journalism. You're certainly doing a good job furthering Inez's career."

He resumed walking without another word, and Grace shuddered. Zeus watched him wide-eyed as he turned the corner. "Gracie," he whispered. "I think that guy might be a vampire."

"He works in talent management, so…yes." Grace wondered at Tristan's comment. If he really had quit because he believed in Inez's right to be a flaky lover, why was he pissed Grace was writing about it?

And why was he even here? Grace hadn't gotten the impression he and Inez were close enough for him to visit her in the hospital.

If Inez and Nelson quit talking to her, she might never know. She put a hand on Zeus's shoulder. "Come on, let's get out of this haunted castle."

As they came out into the balmy, smoggy twilight, Gary,

the Karma Korn fan who had posed for awkward pictures with Inez, stood by the entry, his thin hair plastered to his forehead with sweat. He stared at them like they were giant, murderous cockroaches.

He came forward with jerky steps, his fleshy lips puckered in a frown. "You're those friends of Inez Carter's," he accused.

Grace and Zeus to stepped closer to one another. "Hi," Grace said. "Gary, right?"

Gary's tiny eyes glittered as they darted to the hospital entrance. "Is it true? Is she in there? Inez?"

"Uh…"

Zeus watched the little man with morbid fascination, as if he were watching a pair of hairless cats in the act of copulation. "Inez isn't here right now, but you can leave a message for her after the beep. Beeeeep."

Gary stomped a discount sneaker. "I know she's in there! I read it on the internet! Being in the hospital is no more than she deserves. She's a fake, lying bitch with no morals or…soul. She has no soul." He stood trembling, his nose whistling with each angry breath.

So someone had already broken the story she was in the hospital. *Oh, well.* "You're blowing this out of proportion, I think," Grace said.

"You've sure got a raging case of the angries," Zeus said. "You should have that checked out."

Gary turned abruptly to face Zeus. "You have no idea

what it's like to believe in someone, to believe that they're there for you, that they'll always stand up for you, only to be let down."

Grace watched a shadow pass over Zeus's face; she knew he was thinking of the parents who had finally abandoned him after a life of neglect.

Gary gave them both a contemptuous look. "I hope Inez dies. And you, too. I'll bet you're in on this little joke with her, pretending she's gay just for attention. I hope you all die!"

He spun on his heels, almost lost his balance, regained it and stalked off into the parking lot on stubby legs, disappearing between the lines of cars.

Zeus watched after him. "Some people have mental problems and don't know how to act."

Grace's gaze followed the little man with a frown. Then she started after him, hunkering down behind the parked cars.

Zeus trotted up beside her. "Oh, I get it," he whispered. "We're playing secret agent." He crouched low behind a BMW, his finger gun held near his temple as he hummed the 007 theme song.

"Shh! Zeus!" Grace peeked out and saw Gary climb into a classic blue Mustang. She raised an eyebrow. She couldn't think of any car less likely to be his. He started the engine and pulled out, Zeus spinning from behind the BMW and firing his imaginary gun at the Mustang as it drove off.

Gracie took note of the license plate when the car stopped at the payment booth, typing the number into her phone's notes app. Zeus stood and dusted off his knees. "You think that little gremlin man is the one who drugged Inez?"

"It's possible."

"But he didn't know she was sick until he read an article about it."

"Or so he says." Grace pocketed her phone, watching the Mustang pull onto the street. "He did say he wished she was dead. I don't know. But I'm going to figure out what happened to Inez. If I'm going to write celebrity gossip articles, I might as well write interesting ones."

And, if she managed to find out who had tried to kill Inez, maybe Nelson would forgive her.

10

Grace was jittery on the drive back home, feeling invisible eyes on her at every stoplight. "I'm just glad that creep hadn't figured out that you're the crush, and I'm the person who wrote the article about it."

"True, that," Zeus replied. "He probably would have hulked out bigtime if he'd known." He kneaded his chin like a stress ball. "Do you really think that little creature had something to do with Inez being drugged? I don't know, Gracie. He doesn't seem like a criminal mastermind."

"Yeah, I don't know either." She worried her bottom lip between her teeth. Zeus's mannerisms were contagious. "He said he read on the internet about her being in the hospital, which means someone already broke the story. That was sure quick."

"Was bound to happen, with how nosy people are these days. It must be because all the nose jobs they get." His eyes grew distant, and he whispered to himself, his eyes opening wider and wider. He turned to Grace, fluttering his hands.

"Gracie, Gracie. I've figured something out. I think plastic surgeons are implanting robotic noses on people that make them nosy, so they'll seek out information on the human race and transmit it back to the mothership!"

Grace glanced at him sidelong. "Well, I can't really rule that out."

Zeus giggled. "And what's the difference between nose jobs and hand jobs, anyway? Am I missing out on something?"

Grace ignored him as he muttered and laughed to himself all the way home.

When they got back to the motel room, Grace opened her laptop. A quick search turned up an article in *Celebrity Life*. It had been posted an hour and a half before, when she and Zeus were on their way to the hospital. It stated briefly that Inez was at Cedars Sinai for treatment of ailments unknown.

The author of the article was Marla Poccino.

"Shit," Grace muttered.

But that wasn't the worst of it. Another article had been posted a little less than an hour later, when they'd been on the way back from the hospital. This one was much longer and had a lot more comments. *Inez Carter Hospitalized for Apparent Suicide Attempt*, the headline read.

"What the hell?" Grace said.

"What's going on, Gracie?" Zeus left off carefully prodding his nose in front of the mirror and plopped down beside her, peeking at the screen.

"They're saying Inez's overdose was a suicide." With painful trepidation, she clicked on the headline.

Inez Carter was admitted to Cedars Sinai for a heroin overdose this evening, the article began. *According to inside sources, the singer was found in her hotel room without a pulse and was revived by paramedics. She is currently in serious but stable condition and continues to be closely monitored by medical personnel.*

One of Ms. Carter's close friends spoke with this reporter about the incident.

"Inez doesn't do heroin," said the friend, who asked to remain anonymous. "I don't think this was a normal overdose. I think this was a suicide attempt. I know Inez was upset about that article in High Note *slandering her, casting doubt on her sexual orientation. It's hard to be an outspoken advocate for the* LGBTQ+ *community. She takes a lot of abuse for that, and she's also been under so much stress as she finishes her upcoming album* Spirit Shopper. *I think that article was the last straw."*

"Oh my fucking God," Grace said. She pressed the heels of her hands into her eyes for a full thirty seconds. "Is this for real?"

"My senses tell me it is," Zeus said, his eyes fixed on the screen.

It got worse. The piece mentioned Grace by name as the author of the supposedly slanderous article. It went on to say that there were hopes Inez would recover and get back into the studio in the following weeks.

In order to raise awareness of Inez' struggles, which mirror those of many in the LGBTQ+ community who find themselves under attack because of their orientation, the band has decided to pre-release a single from the upcoming album. It's entitled How You Make Me Feel. *The song is about learning to love yourself and persevere through great opposition, even when social convention and public opinion are against you. The band thought it was appropriate to release the single now at a time when it might be of comfort to Inez, bolster her confidence, and remind her that, even when she's brought low by the cruel words of small-minded people, she's strong enough to withstand it.*

You have legions of supporters, Inez. You're not alone. You can get through this, and so can all the other people suffering oppression and discrimination.

Please show your support for Inez Carter by tweeting with the hashtag #WeLoveInezTheLez, and by purchasing her new single, The Way You Make Me Feel, *available this Tuesday.*

Grace wasn't surprised to see the name at the bottom of the article: again, Marla Poccino.

"Shit," Grace spat. "That little snarky, green-eyed twit is like my archnemesis." She closed the article, not wanting to look at it another moment longer. Grace was going to pay hell for this.

With trembling fingers, she logged into her Twitter account, and immediately wished she hadn't. The hashtag #WeLoveInezTheLez was trending. When she pulled up Inez's feed, most of the recent comments were spewing bile about Grace's article. Grace herself had hundreds of notifications and more were pouring in every second; on a normal day, she'd get maybe three or four.

Her mouth went dry. People were calling her a fraud, a homophobe, and worse. "If you killed Inez Carter, I'm going to kill YOU, @GraceMorgan," one of them said. Plenty more were variations on that theme.

Her stomach curled up against her ribs and called in sick for the day. "Shit, shit, *shit*," she groaned.

Zeus leaned his chin on her shoulder as he read. "Whoa, Gracie, the internet is taking a dump on you for real."

She nodded, fighting back tears. "That's the truth."

"That's complete non-*sense*." He stared at the screen as if he'd like to jump through it and beat the words into a pulp. Grace felt roughly the same way.

"But the worst thing is," Grace said with a sinking feeling, "it had to be Nelson who gave Marla the info for that article."

Zeus's brow furrowed. "Really?"

"Who else would it be? He tipped her off that Inez was in the hospital, and then when he got angry at me for writing the article, he concocted this bullshit and fed it to her."

Zeus tapped his fingers against his lips. "Couldn't it have been that vampire we altercated with in the hallway? Vampires do stuff like that. They love a good Twitter bloodbath."

Gracie thought about it. "But why?"

"Any publicity is good publicity."

"But Tristan doesn't even work for Duke anymore—Nelson told me. He quit after the rave."

"He doesn't?" Zeus's head bobbed back and forth as he pondered, then he shrugged. "Maybe he just did it for fun, then."

Grace snorted. "Some fun."

Zeus gave her a sympathetic smile. "I don't know for sure who did it, but this doesn't smell like Nelson. It has a sort of synthetic, Judas tang that doesn't jive with his hippie musk."

Grace crossed her arms over her chest, wishing she could believe that. No other explanation made sense. She'd known Nelson was pissed, but not *this* pissed. She'd obviously misread him from the beginning.

Zeus watched her closely as the decisiveness in her stance grew. "If he really *did* do it, fuck that little bitch. And I don't need Inez, either." He grinned brightly and pulled Grace into a hug so tight she worried her liver would rupture like an over-stressed water balloon.

"We're gonna be okay, Gracie," he said as she struggled to breathe. "You'll keep writing your articles, and you'll come with me when I go on tour, and everything will work out fantagulastically. This story will end with glorious, flashy, Broadway fanfare, everyone smiling and tap-dancing and singing a happy song, fireworks going off, showgirls doing their kicks. You'll see."

Grace wiggled from his arms with great effort and filled her newly liberated lungs with air. "Thanks, Zeus."

Her phone rang. She and Zeus exchanged a half-fearful look as she picked it up. She cringed and cursed when she saw the number, then hit the answer icon. "Hey, Lawrence."

"How you doing, Grace?" He gave a hollow little laugh. "Looks like your article stirred up something."

She closed her eyes, fighting off a headache and the knowledge of her quickly impending doom. "Yeah, I guess it did. But I was just telling the truth."

There was a short silence. "Is that so?" His tone was guarded.

"Yes, Lawrence. I went to this party, and Inez Carter was ignoring her girlfriend and flirting with a man."

"Are you sure that's what you saw, Grace?"

"*Yes*, Lawrence."

"Because this *Celebrity Life* article makes you out as a liar and a homophobe, both very serious accusations in this social climate and not an image *High Note* wants to be associated with. Plus, being accused of causing someone to commit suicide because of slander, well…"

Bile rose into Grace's throat. "I'm *sure of what I saw*, Lawrence. Every word of the article is true. I'm not entirely certain yet why Inez is in the hospital, but I do know she didn't try to overdose because of my article." She stopped short of telling him she'd been in the hospital with the singer. He'd wonder why she hadn't broken the story herself, and it was too complicated to explain right now. It would just make her seem like a bigger liar.

"Okay," Lawrence said, and she could tell he didn't really believe her. "I just wanted to make sure. Sometimes people can misinterpret things."

"I didn't," she insisted. "Not this time."

"Good enough. But if you can't make this right, Grace, if you can't get another article clarifying and supporting what you said about Inez Carter, we're going to have to print a retraction, saying that you'd made a mistake and apologizing for the pain you caused. I'm sorry, but the editors just don't want the controversy right now."

Grace had to wrestle her stomach into submission. "I understand. I'll work on another article."

"Good." The phone rasped against Lawrence's chin. Grace could picture him squirming. "And, I'm sorry to have to do this to you, but we need it within five days. Otherwise, we feel our reputation will be too damaged. We'll put out a notice that we're investigating these allegations, and we'll need to follow up on that soon or people will say we're blowing smoke to cover our asses."

Grace felt like someone had crashed her head between a pair of cymbals. *How the fuck am I going to do this in five days?* "Okay," she said mechanically. "Five days. No problem."

They said their goodbyes—there was no invitation to drinks this time—and Grace tossed the phone down and flopped onto her face on the bed. "Shit," she spat into her pillow. "My career is over."

Zeus plopped down next to her, hard enough that she bounced like a ping-pong ball on the spring mattress. "What's up?"

"I have five days to figure out this mess with Inez and write another article. If I don't, *High Note* is going to publish a piece saying I was lying about her not being one-hundred-percent Grade A Gay."

To top that off, her former contacts were now working with her pert-butted enemy. How was she supposed to get an article if no one would talk to her?

Zeus tapped a syncopated rhythm on her back with his fingertips. "You can do it, Gracie. You're smart and you'll figure it out."

She turned over and stared up at him helplessly. "How?"

He continued his rhythm on her stomach. "I don't know. Maybe you could call Nelson and try to work it out with him. You could have him confirm on the record that Inez tongue-kissed me like a cute little dog trying to lick peanut butter from my back teeth."

Grace fought off that image, only to have it replaced by the even less palatable one of Nelson's expression when they'd left the hospital. She shook her head listlessly. "I don't think that's going to work, Zeus."

"Well, find Gary the Gnome, then, and subject him to a medieval interrogation. Like you said, he might be the one who overdosed her, and if you can get him to admit that, BAM! Article!" He gave her belly an extra hard smack.

"Ouch! Zeus!"

He hung his head. "Sorry. I forgot you weren't a drum." He went back to tapping her more lightly.

She thought about the Gary connection, and snorted. "The only thing that would come of talking to Gary is I'd catch his head cold, probably. Why would he admit he'd attempted to murder his former hero? I don't think he'd even talk to me to begin with. He was pretty mad at the hospital."

"I'm sure he'd love the chance to have his anger published for the whole world to see. People love to splatter their feelings on other people's faces, and the more people the better. And sometimes when they're doing the splattering, things come out that they don't expect."

Grace gnawed on the inside of her cheek. She didn't have anything to lose by following the lead, no matter how tenuous it was "You know, you might be right. I should talk to him."

"Yep. You're a writer, but I'm a righter. Get it?" Grace rolled her eyes as Zeus grabbed her by the hand and pulled her up off the bed. "But first, let's go get some fancy cupcakes. You know how you like fancy cupcakes. Maybe if you put some of those in your belly, it will recharge your brain with fabulous cupcake power and help get this article written in a flash."

Grace didn't think a cupcake would solve the mystery of why Inez Carter was really in the hospital, but she *was* in desperate need of a sugar high. They went to a bakery down the street, and Grace ended up purchasing an entire coconut cream cake. It put her further into debt, but she told herself that you had to spend money to make money.

They ate the cake on their beds while watching a rerun of *Mythbusters*. Zeus babbled through the entire program, cheering and bouncing up and down every time something exploded, but Grace hardly watched at all. She sucked frosting off her fork and entered Gary's license number into a background search.

It came up with an address in Thousand Oaks. She put down her plate of half-eaten cake and glanced at the clock. It was seven p.m. on a Saturday. Everybody with any sort of social life was currently out enjoying it. So Gary should be home.

"I'm going to visit Gary right now," she said.

Zeus shoveled down his last bite of cake, which was the size of a softball; he had to work it down like a snake swallowing a bunny. That accomplished, he gasped, "I'm going with you."

Grace arranged her expression into blankness, imagining Zeus swinging from the curtain rods while she tried to interview Gary. "That's okay, Zuzu. I can handle it on my own."

"Don't be silly. There's no way I'm going to let you joust that foe without me. He'll probably gas you and pin you to a cork board with his other female specimens."

Grace fidgeted with her fork. When she gave it more thought, taking Zeus didn't seem like a completely ludicrous idea. Considering who she'd be dealing with, the vibe couldn't be made much weirder by the addition of her foster son. Besides, the idea of dealing with Gary alone creeped her out.

People tended to judge Zeus harshly, but that was their problem, not hers. Besides, maybe having someone of Zeus's temperament along would make the interview seem less formal. Not like someone investigating an attempted murder, but like a friendly visit from acquaintances.

That gave Grace an idea. She smiled at Zeus. "Okay, then. Let's go."

Zeus bounded out the door like a puppy excited about going walkies. Grace grabbed her purse and followed with less enthusiasm, regretting her decision to feed him so much sugar.

On the drive, Zeus rummaged in the glove box, finding a rumpled note pad covered in coffee stains and an ancient pen. He tucked a curly lock behind his ear. "What questions should we ask him? I'm going to start with why…are you… such…a…schnozberry?"

The pen scratched laboriously over the paper. He dotted the question mark violently and chewed the end of the pen. "What else? Oh yes. Why…do you smell…like… goat…balls?"

Grace tapped her fingertips on the steering wheel as they waited in traffic, thinking they might as well ask Gary those questions, for all the good this interview would probably do. She'd never done any sort of interrogation before; hard-hitting investigative journalism was outside her normal scope. She'd mostly covered arts and entertainment, the Seattle music scene.

Right before she'd been laid off, the paper had added local news reporting to her duties. It had mostly involved sleeping through city council meetings and talking to the police about sensational or weird crimes. She'd never really gotten the hang of it.

She could daydream all she wanted about a dramatic confession or a foot chase through the streets of Thousand Oaks, with herself as the kickass female hero who ran him down, tackled him, and handed him over to police. A story like that would certainly get her off the hook with *High Note*, and possibly with Nelson. But Grace knew she and good luck weren't on speaking terms these days.

The address she'd gotten from the database was in a development of tidy beige-stucco houses, all of them slightly deformed clones of some California Bland Suburban Bungalow. The house number Grace was looking for was easily visible in the twilight, illuminated by the warm glow of a cut crystal carriage lamp and encircled by a riot of red bougainvillea. Sure enough, the blue Mustang was parked in the driveway. At least she'd located the man in question. Unfortunately, that wasn't the hard part.

Grace parked along the curb, wondering whether Gary lived with rich parents. She imagined a pair of older Garies peering at her like chameleons trying to blend in with a backdrop of beige accent walls and shuddered.

She and Zeus climbed out into the balmy evening air. HOA-approved palm trees rustled in the faint breeze. Zeus clutched his notepad and gave Grace a grim nod. "Let's rake this perp over the coals."

She opened her mouth to give him a lecture on appropriate behavior, then closed it again, shrugged, and followed him up the cobblestone walk.

She turned on her cell phone voice recorder before stowing it back in her purse, just in case Gary did blurt out a full confession like on *Murder She Wrote*.

Light spilled through the frosted glass flanking the arched wooden door. Zeus's lips moved as he gave his notes a last perusal, and Grace paused on the doorstep, her heart pounding. How had a story about a celebrity's love life turned into an attempted murder investigation? She felt like a Girl Scout asked to pull off a mob hit during a cookie-hawking expedition. Wiping the sweat from the back of her neck, she rang the bell.

Chimes sounded inside, and a shadow moved behind the frosted glass. The door opened, revealing a six-foot-tall, ebony-skinned hunk in a Decemberists T-shirt. He smiled, regarding them with polite bewilderment through his square-framed glasses. "Hello there."

Grace blinked. "Uh, hi. We're looking for Gary…?"

"We have a few questions for him about his whereabouts yesterday evening," Zeus added, his attempt at looking like a square-jawed FBI agent foiled somewhat by the coconut cream on his rainbow unicorn t-shirt. Grace gave him a swift kick to the ankle, making him drop his pen.

"I'm Grace Morgan and this is Zeus Mahoney. We're friends of Inez Carter." She hoped this wouldn't hurt their cause. "We ran into Gary at the hospital earlier. He was very upset, and we were wondering if we could speak with him."

The man's gaze lingered on Zeus, who was scrabbling between the potted geraniums for his pen. "I didn't know Inez and Gary had friends in common."

Grace's mouth went dry. "Well, ah…"

"We met a few days ago," Zeus said, straightening and sticking his pen behind his ear. "When we were with Inez." He glanced sideways at Grace.

"He really made an impression," she added quickly. "And Inez…I know Inez wouldn't want a fan like him to be upset with her."

"Her fans are super, duper important to her," Zeus said, catching on, for once.

Grace clutched her purse strap tightly as the man leaned against the doorjamb, examining them. She knew it would look ridiculous to show up at a near-stranger's house with a story like this, but she hadn't really contemplated *how* ridiculous. She was about to apologize and leave, hopefully before she died of embarrassment, when the man nodded.

"Gary told me he ran into you guys at the hospital," he said, and Grace tried to hide her surprise. "This whole thing with Inez has been really hard on him. It might actually help if he talked to you." He stood aside. "Come on in, I'll see if I can get him to come out of his room."

Grace and Zeus exchanged a look of disbelief and stepped into the house.

Gary's house, like his car, was completely at odds with the image Grace had of Gary. It had gleaming hardwood floors and tasteful midcentury modern décor, all of it set off by soft, recessed lighting.

"I'm Miles, by the way," the man said, shaking Grace's hand. His looked again at Zeus, who was inspecting a painting on the wall, his pen scratching on his notepad. Grace second-guessed her decision to bring her friend; she hadn't expected to have to deal with someone as normal-seeming as Miles.

Zeus hooked the picture frame with his pointer finger and gently pulled it back to peek behind. "I'd like to take a look in your secret compartments, please."

Grace winced and prepared to launch into her oft-rehearsed but much-hated "explanation" of Zeus. But before she could, Miles's lips twitched into a half-smile. "Now, slow down, we just met." He winked at Grace and gestured to the living room. "You can go ahead and have a seat. I'll check on Gary."

Grace nodded and watched him disappear down the hallway. *What a nice man.* Maybe his close association with Gary—in what capacity, she wasn't sure yet—made him tolerant of social diversity.

Zeus started rummaging through the drawers of the hall tree, and she grabbed his wrist. "Come on, Zuzu. No clues in there. Let's sit down."

Zeus widened his eyes in protest. "Clues could be *anywhere*, Gracie," he hissed. "I'm sure this place is *infested* with clues. We'll probably have to scrape them off our shoes when we leave."

Grace gave him The Look, and eventually he sighed in resignation. He closed the drawer and followed her into the living room.

Grace settled into a Danish Z chair while Zeus sprawled on the long, blocky sofa. She glanced around at the vintage reproduction television and the abstract found-object collages on the walls. The place looked like a tasteful, upper-class set of *The Jetsons*.

Zeus felt between the couch cushions and peered under the throw pillows. Grace stomped her foot, and he settled sheepishly back on the sofa, demurely replacing a quarter he'd found and folding his hands in his lap.

Gary's voice rang from the back of the house, most of the words indistinct save for "jerkfaces" and "inferiority complex". Miles's soothing tones wove through the pauses. Grace was beginning to regret wasting gas to come listen to a strange little man have a tantrum, when the voices quit and footsteps approached from down the hall.

Gary stomped into the room wearing moccasin slippers and a poorly fastened maroon bathrobe over faded flannel pajamas. Grace wondered why, if he lived in a house like this, he always looked like he shopped off the clearance rack at Sears.

Gary's tiny eyes flashed. His thin lips twisted in a sneer. Miles came up behind him, looking preemptively apologetic.

"Well?" Gary said. "I see you haven't died of your nasty phony bitch disease yet."

Zeus's back straightened, and he opened his mouth. He didn't take well to people calling Grace names.

"It's understandable that you're upset," Grace cut in quickly, before Zeus could get started. "I wanted to talk to you about that, in fact. I'd hoped we could explain the situation a bit more, so you wouldn't be so angry at Inez."

Gary glared, his nostrils gleaming with moisture. "How do you even know where I live?"

Grace fidgeted with the phone hidden in her purse and exchanged a look with Zeus.

"We have our ways," Zeus said, his steely gaze fixed on the little man. "You can't even begin to imagine what we're capable of."

Miles's hand came up to hide a smirk, but Gary actually looked somewhat impressed. Grace took her chance, groping for the right words. "Listen. Inez is a really good person. She's not trying to hurt or mislead anyone. She's just, you know, going through a phase where she explores her sexual orientation." Grace cringed inwardly at how trite that sounded, but it might be approaching the truth.

Gary sniffed. "Another article came up in *Celebrity Life* just now that says Inez actually *is* a lesbian, and that that the article in *High Note* is a lie. The *Celebrity Life* article says Inez tried to commit suicide because she was so upset people were lying about her sexual orientation. But I don't think that's true. I think the second article is just a cover-up, because people are so angry. I've *met* Inez Carter. I've watched all her videos and interviews a million times. I *know* her. She doesn't seem like the type to commit suicide." Gary smugly arranged his grubby bathrobe, pulling it even more askew.

Grace wondered how someone who seemed so socially inept could have come to such an astute conclusion. She also wondered if someone who had poisoned Inez would make this argument. Wouldn't the poisoner *want* people to think it was suicide?

Grace nodded cautiously. "You're right. She's not the type to commit suicide. But Inez had nothing to do with that article. She wasn't trying to cover anything up. It was written by an unscrupulous reporter who just wanted to further her own career by printing lies."

Gary squinted at her, picking at an ingrown hair on his chin.

Grace took a deep breath. "The thing is," she persisted, "we have reason to believe that someone may be trying to hurt Inez. We think she may have been poisoned."

Gary stopped picking and his eyes popped open. "Aha! Now we get to the real reason you're here. Inez doesn't care how I feel about her." He tugged violently at his robe. "You think *I* tried to hurt her! Pish." His scoff misted the air with snot, and he began cleaning his nose elaborately with the sleeve of his robe, holding Grace's gaze steadily throughout the procedure. "That's ridiculous," he muttered. "I don't have time for this."

But he made no move to leave, so Grace plowed ahead. "I'm not saying it was you who tried to hurt her. It's just that you…uh…seem so well-connected to the, you know, the scene around here, and seem to have your finger on the pulse of public sentiment…"

Zeus's pen clunked onto the notepad on his lap. Miles's eyebrows crept up, and he bit his lip. She avoided meeting either of their stares.

Gary didn't see through her inept flattery, however.

His stiff posture began to relax. He finished his perusal of his nostrils and smoothed his greasy forelock. "I don't have any idea who would want to hurt Inez Carter. If she was really poisoned, it was obviously by some mentally ill weirdo, and not me." His eyes bored into Grace like parasitic beetles. "What happened to her? Why do you think someone poisoned her?"

Grace paused, wondering how much she could and should tell these people. But if she didn't build trust and rapport, how could she ever expect to get information from them?

She was beginning to suspect that this was the reason Miles let them in in the first place: the possibility of some hot celebrity gossip would cheer Gary up. She sighed. "Why don't you guys sit down? It's a long story."

Miles and Gary settled into the vintage avocado green velvet chairs flanking the coffee table. They leaned forward with rapt expressions as she told the story of Inez's fight with an unknown Twitter follower, and her supposed overdose. She watched the faces of the two men closely as she spoke; Miles looked perturbed and thoughtful, while Gary absentmindedly picked the scabs from the ghosts of pimples past. Zeus traced the color patterns in the crocheted afghan folded over the back of the couch, his lips moving as he whispered to himself.

When Grace had finished her tale, Gary reclined and threw his arm over the back of his chair. "I think the question is, how would a fan have determined Miss Carter's whereabouts? I believe her agent is Duke Morey? He's usually fairly good at keeping his clients' locations secret."

Grace blinked. He really did his research.

Zeus looked up from the afghan. "Everything's connected, like in this blanket. The question is, what happens when the yarn runs out?"

They all glanced at him briefly, then away again.

"How did you know who Inez's manager was?" Grace asked.

Miles uncrossed and re-crossed his legs, rolling his eyes self-deprecatingly. "Duke is my agent, too, and he happened to mention he'd signed her."

Grace raised her eyebrows. "Oh?"

Gary gestured jerkily at a couple of the collages lining the walls. "Miles is an artist. In fact, he and I met when Duke approached me about a showing at one of my galleries."

Grace nodded. The mystery of why-does-Gary-have-money was solved. And was Miles his boyfriend? Gary and Miles shared a glance of secret amusement, and Grace found that it wasn't as hard for her to picture them as a couple as it was when she'd first walked in. She suspected there was more to Gary than she'd thought. It wasn't right to judge anyone else's relationships. "Is that why you're such a big Karma Korn fan?" she asked. "Because Inez has the same manager as Miles?"

Gary sputtered derisively. "I've followed Inez's career for years. I knew she was headed for greatness since her first album *Binky Boop*. Duke didn't sign Inez until a couple months ago, shortly after she gave that speech at the White House."

Miles and Gary grinned, while Grace and Zeus exchanged a gleeful look.

"Inez's White House speech was epic," Grace said.

Zeus pressed his hands to his mouth and made a loud farting noise, and the others laughed.

Inez had been invited to play at the White House during a conference on youth culture and higher education. After their set, Inez had kept the mic and started asking the President questions about his personal stance on gay marriage. When he'd tried to dodge the question, she'd turned her ass toward him and farted a rough squeaker into the mic. The Secret Service quickly escorted her out, as if her ass were a dangerous weapon she'd been wielding against the President. It had been the true beginning of her career.

Gary's smile faded. He crossed his arms tightly over his chest, which had a pushup bra effect on his little man boobs. "At any rate, whoever it was that drugged Inez must have had inside connections," he said.

"Or was really good at internet stalking," mused Miles.

Grace chewed her lip. Zeus looked back and forth between Gary and Miles, making motions in the air as if he were crocheting the two men together.

"Whoever it was, it certainly wasn't *me*," Gary said. The heels of his slippers flapped as he stomped.

Grace nodded. "Do you have any idea who it might have been? There was no one else in your circle who was upset about the article in *High Note?*"

Gary gestured wildly. "Quite a few of us were upset about it, of course."

Miles leaned back in his chair. "We don't know anyone upset enough to murder about it, though. I mean, if that article is true, sure, it's a little cheesy to be promoted as one of the spokespeople for the LGBTQ community, only to then have it discovered you're lying about your sexual orientation. That narrative just feeds those who believe being gay is just a phase, or something you can be cured of."

"But the truth is, sometimes it is a sort of discovery phase," Grace said. "People should have room to explore that, too. Some people think they're only attracted to one gender and then find out later they're attracted to all of them. It happens."

"Being who you are is one of the things the LGBTQ community is all about," Zeus piped in. "Inez is just being the crazy cosmic cat that she is, and not who her fans think she should be."

Gary huffed, but Miles nodded. "If she's bi or pan or whatever, I think people will come around and accept it, once the furor dies down. If Inez comes out and is honest about what she's going through, it will end up adding to the conversation instead of detracting from it, and the community can't really be angry about that."

Miles studied Grace, a smile growing on his lips. "You're the one who wrote that article, aren't you?" His eyes flicked to Zeus. "And this is the guy…"

Gary's back jerked so straight Grace worried he might rocket through the textured ceiling. "You're Grace Morgan? And this is Zeus Mahoney?"

Grace clutched her purse strap. Zeus went perfectly still, staring at Gary, then threw the afghan over his head and began bleating like a burglar alarm.

"Hush, Zeus!" Grace ordered.

Zeus bleated more quietly.

Miles hid his face in his hands and turned away, his shoulders shaking with laughter.

Gary's expression didn't change at all, however. He kept staring at Grace with unnerving intensity, blinking even less than usual.

Grace sighed. "Yeah, that's us."

Miles took his hands from his face, drying his eyes on his t-shirt. Grace clutched the pointed armrests, waiting for Gary to explode and kick them out.

But he didn't. His eyes glittered as he continued to stare, and he leaned toward Grace. "So, is it true, then? What you said about Inez liking…him?" He jerked his weak chin at

Zeus, who had stopped bleeping and was whispering and poking his fingers through the holes in the afghan.

Grace shrugged reluctantly. "Yeah, it's true. I didn't mean to start such a firestorm, though. Inez isn't a bad person. We just can't help who we're attracted to, I guess."

Zeus peeked out from under the blanket, then wrapped it around his head. "My sexiness transcends sexual orientation and causes sexual disorientation."

Miles cleared his throat. "That happens sometimes."

Gary fixated on Zeus. Grace tensed, wondering if she would have to defend her friend from the man's snot-flinging wrath. But instead, Gary rested his elbows on his knees. "Tell me about Lyssa Medlin. Is it true she once took too many mushrooms and was in the hospital for three days, thinking she'd turned into a hot air balloon?"

Grace let out a quiet sigh of relief, catching Miles's knowing smirk.

Zeus pulled the blanket tighter around his face. "I don't know. We just climbed on to the friendship train together, so we're still learning about each other's drug habits and such. I sure hope so, though, because being a hot air balloon would be really interesting and I want her to tell me about it someday."

They stayed for another half hour. Gary grilled them about all their celebrity contacts and told them an intricately detailed story about the time he'd met Angelina Jolie. They finally escaped, Gary giving them his card and inviting them to come see his galleries. Grace couldn't help but feel a little flattered that he thought they were well-connected enough to latch onto.

As they drove away, though, dull frustration took over. She switched off her phone recorder with a violent jab. "Well, I'm no closer to figuring out what happened. Gary doesn't seem like he's the one."

"Every mystery needs a red herring," Zeus said, sticking Gary's card into the frame around the sun visor mirror. He giggled. "Wouldn't it be weird, though, if the red herring was actually whodunit this time?"

Grace gazed out the windshield and quirked her lips. "Could be. I mean, like they said, it has to be someone who's pissed off at Inez and either well-connected or good at stalking. Gary seems to follow Inez around everywhere, and he knows her manager, so he'd have access to information like what hotel she was staying in, if he could get it out of Duke somehow."

Grace pulled onto the 101. Maybe Gary *was* a criminal mastermind and a genius at the art of deception. She pounded her steering wheel and cursed. "This case needs a frigging detective, and I'm a goddamn music journalist."

Zeus ruffled her hair. "We'll crack this case, Detective Morgan, no worries." He began dancing in his seat and scatting the theme from *Law and Order*.

Grace stared bleakly at the line of taillights in front of her. *I have to crack this case. Either I'm good enough to solve this mystery and bag this story, or I'm doomed to be a failure, someone who isn't good enough at the job she loves to even afford her own apartment.*

mystery and bag this story, or I'm doomed to be a failure, someone who isn't good enough at the job she loves to even afford her own apartment.

11

That night Grace dreamt that her ex-husband showed up at her motel room with Marla Poccino.

"We brought you some things," Marla said, smiling sweetly and opening a huge shopping bag. She pulled out a gigantic, gilt statue of a smiling Buddha. "This would look great next to your bed, don't you think?" Marla wrangled it into position. "It will cover up this stain on the wall." She delved again into the bag, retrieving a huge computer tablet in a gaudy frame. She took down Grace's college diploma, which was hanging on the motel wall for some reason, and put the tablet in its place. Marla punched the power button, and the screen began displaying stock market information. In the bottom right corner, an inset video gave a tutorial about how not to get grape slushie in your hair, with advice on better ways to style it.

"Now you can keep an eye on your investments while you sit here waiting for work," Marla said.

Mitch leaned against the wall smirking. Rage bubbled up in Grace like magma. He knew quite well that she had no investments: he'd liquidated or hidden them before their divorce, a fact which had left her without enough money for a good lawyer to prove it in court.

The stock market display flashed off, replaced by the slick smile of an anchorwoman. "We have breaking news on the apparent attempt on singer Inez Carter's life," she said.

Marla stepped in front of the screen, an expression of false concern on her face. "Is there anything else we can do for you?"

Grace tried to step around her and see the report, but Marla kept moving to block her view.

"We just feel so bad that you've ended up like this," Marla said.

"Move, I need to see this," Grace said, trying to push her aside.

Mitch came to put his arm around Marla, further blocking the screen. "We really want you to succeed," he said. "That's why we had Zeus put in an institution, so he wouldn't be a distraction while you try to find work."

These words cut through Grace's frustration, and her heart stalled. "You *what?*"

"Put him away," Mitch said. "In an institution. They'll do a better job of caring for him there than you can, and it will give you time to concentrate on getting a real job."

Fury exploded white hot in Grace's skull. She lunged at them, trying to grab both their throats at once.

She woke up screaming, flailing underneath the thin quilt.

"Shhh, it's okay, Gracie."

"Fuck you, you twatfaced cuntnuggets!"

"Hush, Gracie, or the language police will come."

The scream died in her throat, and she lay panting, lights flashing behind her eyes as the dream faded into the dark motel room. Orange stripes of streetlight splashed over the hulky furniture. Zeus scrambled up from where he'd been curled at her feet (which he still sometimes did during times of stress) and curled against her chest instead.

"Bad day in the dream dimensions?" he muttered sleepily. "Having trouble with some cuntnugget or other?"

Her heartbeat gradually slowed as her anger faded. She tried to scoot away from Zeus, but he just scooted with her until her butt was hanging off the edge of the mattress. "Zeus," she complained, but he was already snoring.

Grace sighed. Him crowding her in bed was better than him being in the mental hospital, at least.

After a few minutes, she realized she wasn't likely to get back to sleep, anyway. She gently eased herself out of bed and brewed a cup of instant coffee in the microwave. The noise caused Zeus to toss over in his sleep and mutter something about the resonant frequency of Satan.

The bedside clock gleamed a dull red: 2:23 in the morning. She rubbed the grit from her eyes, gulped down some strong coffee, and flipped open her laptop.

Ignoring her own menacing notifications, she pulled up Inez's Twitter account and scrolled through the thousands upon thousands of mentions and direct tweets, looking for the interaction with the upset fan Inez had remembered having before she lost consciousness. Most of the tweets mentioning her profile wished Inez a speedy recovery and expressed support, though there were plenty that called her a junky lesbo bitch, and some that were just unintelligible. *I got 2 find your @InezCarter earwig their on your brain,* one of them said, and Grace read through it about fifteen times before realizing she was wasting her time trying to find a clue there.

As she reached the replies time stamped around eight the previous evening, before Marla's article had posted, the comments tapered off and their character changed, with more of them being the usual pleas for attention that all celebrities received. *It's my birthday, @InezCarter, can I get a RT??*

Inez had duly retweeted and had responded with a demure *Happy birthday! Thanks for being such a great fan!*

Grace's fingers tapped the keys bemusedly. She tried to imagine Inez typing such a trite message. She couldn't. Maybe the star had a bot responding to birthday tweets, or a publicist.

She kept scrolling. There were more ats from fans, with more generic responses from Inez, and some from non-fans, calling her names or quoting bible verses, telling her she was a rot on society and such. But Grace couldn't find any death threats. None of the negative ats had responses from Inez's account at all.

Grace was about to give up, thinking that the death threat must have been a direct message or hallucination, when she got to the tweets that were time-stamped ten hours ago, and saw something that piqued her interest.

Listening to @KarmaKorn's Manic Dream Life, the tweet said. *You're the other half of my soul peanut, @InezCarter.*

What was interesting was Inez' response: *@KatOnTinRufies Mmmm, soul peanuts. We should eat each other.*

Now *that* sounded like the real Inez.

Grace read on and found more responses in Inez's whacked-out style. *I'll keep a tongue out for you, hot lips,* was the response to an L.A. fan saying she'd heard Inez was in town and would keep an eye out for her. And, to a guy who sent her a selfie of his bare-chested reflection in the mirror saying it would turn her straight, Inez responded, *My mom has better tits than you.*

Then Grace came to another conversation, and her heartbeat accelerated.

I know what hotel you're staying in, @InezCarter, the message said. *I have a friend that works there & told me. I'm coming for you.*

Come on over, @CharlizeAngel, Inez had responded. *I'll bake you a cunt cake.*

"Yes!" Grace exclaimed. Zeus flopped over in his sleep, and Grace put a hand over her mouth. It was now four in the morning, and she was celebrating that someone had gotten an internet death threat—one that Grace herself might have inadvertently inspired, no less. She rubbed her eyes, sighed, and read on.

The conversation had started with a tweet by @CharlizeAngel: *I read an article in* High Note *saying @InezCarter is faking being gay. That's an insult to those who really are.*

Grace bit back her guilt and read on. *WTF are you talking about?* Inez responded.

You know exactly what I'm talking about. You're faking being gay because it's trendy now, and you think it will sell your music.

That's bullshit, Inez wrote. *You can probably smell the pussy on my breath from wherever you are.*

I'm not that far from you and I can't smell anything. You're exploiting LGBTQ culture for profit. You're a fake bitch.

Grace's brow furrowed. *Fake bitch.* Wasn't that pretty much what Gary had said? Grace decided it was too generic of a comment to be truly incriminating, but she filed the information away for further thought.

The thread continued, degenerating from there until it ended with Inez's cunt cake comment.

Grace frowned, reading through the thread again and again. Idle internet death threats were a dime a dozen, but had this person somehow followed through with it? Had they managed to make it look like Inez had overdosed? It was just so damned *unlikely.* It was much more likely that

Inez was lying about having taken heroin intentionally.

Grace rubbed her sore neck. She needed more inside info regarding Inez's drug habits. Nelson might not be talking to her any longer, and Inez probably wasn't either, but there was someone else Grace could contact. Someone she'd actually been wanting to speak with all along: Nicole Watters.

Had Grace been too high at the party to establish a good connection? She'd spent about half of their conversation making wawwooowoooaw and bluh-dink-dink noises, trying to imitate a Yamaha DX7 synthesizer's best settings.

If that hadn't been enough to sour Nicole's opinion of her, Inez or Nelson might have warned Nicole not to talk to Grace. It was also likely that Nicole herself was upset about the article. But Grace had to try something. She could hear the timer ticking, and if she didn't get a follow-up article soon the alarm would sound, indicating that her career's goose was fully cooked.

She hadn't had the wherewithal to get Nicole's number or email at the party, so Grace went to the DJ's website. On the contact page, it instructed the press to direct all inquiries to her agent, and Grace's heart squelched: it was Duke Morey, the same salad-eating dorkface who represented both Inez and Miles. What were the odds? Duke must have the whole county on contract.

The agent likely wouldn't be too happy about her *High Note* article, either, and there was very little chance he'd return her call. Resignedly, she closed the tab and brought up Nicole's Twitter account, instead.

To her relief, Grace saw they were following each other; she recalled their late-night party conversations somehow leading to exchanging Twitter handles. The DJ probably got hundreds of DMs a day, but Grace didn't know what else to do. She quickly jotted off a request that the artist call her, then turned off her laptop and flopped down on the bed.

Grace felt the riptide of her life sucking her away from any hope of success. As dawn cast its gray light through the crack in the dusty motel curtains, she wondered how much longer she could stay afloat.

**

Later that morning, Grace went to her P.O. box and found the check from *High Note* waiting, payment for the ill-fated article. At least they'd paid her, but she had to fight back a pang of nausea as she folded the check carefully into her wallet.

She mulled it over as she left the post office. There was no point in putting a deposit down on an apartment in L.A. if her career was ruined. She'd use all the money to pay down her credit card, instead. If she somehow landed a follow-up article, she'd find an apartment. If she couldn't land one, though…Grace quickly pushed away images of having to rely fully on Zeus to support her (his SSI checks were a scant handful of hundreds; not even *one* person could live on disability, much less two, even in rural nowheresville, much less L.A.) or moving back in with her parents. There would be time enough to deeply ponder all her unsavory options if and when they actually became her only options.

She checked her phone every ninety seconds as she went to the bank and the supermarket, but received no Twitter message from Nicole, no email, no phone call; only hundreds upon hundreds of hateful tweets from Inez's fans and supporters. They told her she should hand in her press credentials and probably her vagina as well, as she almost certainly wouldn't be needing either of them anymore.

She slumped back through the door into the motel and threw the bag of groceries onto the table. Zeus looked up from his pushup position in front of the TV. "You hear from the fancy-pants DJ yet?" He'd awoken before she'd left, and Grace had filled him in on how she'd spent the early morning.

She shook her head.

Zeus sprang up and began pawing through the grocery sack. "I think what we need to do is go to more parties, meet more friends. You're sure to get the scoop on what's going on with Inez sooner or later, because everyone knows everyone in Hollywood. Maybe you'll get an even more interesting story."

"Hopefully my popularity will go from leper-with-halitosis to international-rock-star level by this evening, then. I'm not exactly swimming in party invitations, and I have four days to figure this out."

Zeus pulled a bag of mixed salad from the groceries and tore it open, shoving a handful of lettuce in his mouth.

"They're like rabbit potato chips," he said through a mouthful as he crunched them. "Do you think rabbits eat this stuff at their rabbit parties?"

"Rabbits being one of the numerous groups that don't invite me to their parties, I don't know." Grace held up a bottle of soy ginger dressing. "Want some dip with it?"

"No way, I don't want to clog myself up with bad oils." Zeus turned his attention to the cooking show on television, doing squats while he ate.

Grace mulled over her next move as she arranged perishable items Tetris-like in the mini fridge. Should she try calling Duke, in another attempt to contact Nicole? Should she call Nelson and beg him to forgive her? Neither of those options seemed very promising. Part of her longed to call Nelson even so, but her pride wouldn't allow it.

She was trying to drop the block of cheese into the last available slot between the yogurt and half & half when her phone rang.

She tossed aside the cheddar and snatched her cell from her back pocket. The screen displayed a number she didn't know with an L.A. area code.

Grace jabbed the answer icon. "Hello?"

"Hey. Is this Grace Morgan?"

The voice was quiet and female, and Grace's palms started to sweat. "Yes, this is she."

"This is Nicole. I got your message on Twitter."

Grace's knees almost gave out. "Thank you so much for calling back."

Zeus stopped mid-squat to watch her, and Grace gave him the thumbs-up. Zeus threw up his arms and grinned, a movement which made him fall with a thump onto his butt.

"I assume you want to talk to me about Inez being in the hospital?" Nicole said.

"Yes," Grace said. "Something about the *Celebrity Life* article just doesn't seem right, and I'm trying to figure out what really happened."

"Yeah, I know what you mean. Inez doesn't do heroin, and she's not going to go all emo because of some stupid comment in some article, either. But…." Nicole sighed. "Listen, you're a really nice person, and I know you mean well and all, but I don't think I should talk to you. I don't have any information that would help you, and frankly, if my fan base found out I was talking to you, they'd eat me alive. You've been well and truly canceled."

Grace swallowed. "I know you're probably not happy about what I said about Inez in that article. I was just reporting the truth, though."

There was a pause. "Well, Inez is a complicated person, and I don't pretend to own her whole heart."

A knock sounded at the motel door as Grace tried to pick apart Nicole's guarded tone. Grace glanced at Zeus, who was propped up against the wall in some convoluted yoga pose, and jerked her chin at him. He disentangled himself and went over to open the door.

"But Inez's official stance is that she doesn't like men at all," Grace said into the phone. "That doesn't appear to be true. Not that it really matters to me, it just seems odd."

Zeus opened the door on a uniformed package delivery guy with a box and a bouquet of flowers. Grace's brow furrowed, but she turned her attention back to Nicole. "Anyway, all that's beside the point, really. What I'm saying is, I never meant to hurt Inez. I was writing an article about Zeus, and I put the part in about Inez as a point of interest, nothing more. I was telling the truth as I saw it. I guess I should have realized it would be a bigger deal than I thought it was, though, and I'm really sorry."

Zeus closed the door and tore the paper off the package. Grace turned away. They must be a present from Inez. It's good she wasn't punishing Zeus for Grace's article, at least.

"I know you didn't mean to hurt Inez," Nicole said. "And I know you were reporting the truth. I was there when Inez threw herself at Zeus, after all."

"That couldn't have been fun for you to witness," Grace said. "Nothing against Inez, but that was a jerky thing for her to do to you."

Nicole chuckled dryly. "She can do jerky things, it's true." Nicole sighed. "Look. I like you. This situation is effed up, but you're a good person. And you have some seriously good taste in electronic keyboard noises."

A smile grew on Grace's lips, and hope began to filter into her heart. "Thanks." There was another pause, which Grace let hang, trying not to get her hopes up too high.

"Okay," Nicole finally said. "I'll talk to you. Though like I said, I don't know how much help I can be."

Grace threw her fist in the air and mouthed, *Yes!* Zeus looked up from the box, which was full of candy, and gave her a chocolatey grin.

"Thank you so much," Grace said.

"I'll meet you at Danine's Bakery in an hour and answer all your questions as best I can."

"Cool. I'll see you then." Grace hung up and did a little dance. "Yes, yes, yes, I got an interview!"

Zeus put down the box of chocolates, wrapping Grace in a sticky hug. "Yay, Gracie! We're on the upswing of this roller coaster ride. And also, Nelson sent you some nice presents of the type that men typically apologize with, so I'm guessing he's apologizing, though I didn't read the card."

Grace's dancing came to an abrupt halt. "That was from Nelson?!"

"That's what it said on the package."

She wrested herself from Zeus's hug and went over to inspect the gifts: a now half-eaten box of chocolates and a bouquet of red roses. There was a card hanging from the neck of the flower vase, which said *To Grace, From Nelson* on the tiny envelope. She ripped it open, giving Zeus a dirty look. "Why did you open the chocolates if they were for me?"

Zeus blinked. "It's *chocolate*, Gracie."

"What happened to the bad oils?" Grace muttered. She opened the card. Inside was a computer-printed message in an elaborately-loopy cursive font that made her eyes hurt; Nelson must be sorry enough to have gone insane if he chose it deliberately.

Grace, it read, *I'm sorry I was a jerk. I should never have doubted the motives of a woman as beautiful as you. Please accept my apology.*

- Nelson

Grace stared at the message. ...*should never have doubted the motives of a woman as beautiful as you.* Not that she didn't appreciate the sentiment, but what the hell did that even mean?

"Gracie," Zeus said.

She looked on the back of the card, but there was nothing else on there.

"Gracie."

"What is it, Zeus?"

"Gracie, I don't...."

There was a horrible splattering noise behind her, and she turned just in time to see Zeus collapse in a puddle of his own vomit.

12

Grace sat in the back of the ambulance as it sped toward the hospital. A pair of medics, one male and one female, worked on Zeus, their faces hard with concentration.

"Does he have an allergy to chocolate?" the female asked, as she hooked an oxygen mask over Zeus' slack face.

"No allergies that I know of," Grace said shakily. Her tears fell on the box of candy clutched in her hands. The box Nelson had sent her, which somehow had made Zeus keel over. Dulled anger and confusion pounded at her, but they seemed far away.

"Did he take anything? Drugs? Alcohol? Medication?"

Grace shook her head. "He's on medication, but I dole it out to him so he doesn't forget, and it doesn't do this to him."

The EMTs both glanced at her briefly before going back to their work.

"What's wrong with him?" Grace asked hoarsely. "Is he going to be okay?"

"That's what we're trying to figure out."

Then one of the monitors beeped.

"I'm losing the pulse," the female medic said.

Grace whimpered in anguish, trying to breathe. The EMTs hands flew as they worked, speaking to each other in low, clipped jargon that Grace couldn't understand. She squeezed her eyes shut and began to pray to whatever God might listen to a person who had never prayed before in her life.

The ride to the hospital seemed longer than an amateur opera. Grace watched the monitors and the medics through a haze of tears, trying to figure out what was going on and hoping against hope as they gave Zeus CPR and injections. She wanted to ask if he was still alive, but the words wouldn't come. She was afraid to know, and she was powerless to save him, so it did her no good to know. She could only cling to her belief that he would live, and that the universe wouldn't be so stark and pointless to take away someone so good, so innocent, and who had faced so many hardships in his young life.

The monitor's alarm stopped buzzing just before they pulled up to the hospital. The EMTs started barking more jargon at each other.

"Is he okay?" Grace yelped, as a serious-looking doctor opened the back doors to the ambulance.

"We got his heartbeat back," the male EMT said, shooting her a sharp look. "We'll do everything we can. First we need to figure out what he took. This looks like an overdose."

Zeus's neck wobbled as they unfolded the legs of the gurney onto the pavement. "He didn't take anything!" Grace said. Frantic anger took her over. Was Zeus going to die because they didn't believe her? "He's not on drugs. He was just eating the chocolate someone sent me." She looked at the box in her hands, wanting to fling it away from her.

The EMTs wheeled Zeus into the ER. Grace sat dumbly in the back of the ambulance, trembling. She wanted to run after them, but her legs didn't seem to work.

"Miss Morgan?"

She glanced up, startled, and saw a man peering at her, his clean-shaven jowls weirdly illuminated by late morning sunlight mixed with the flashing lights of the ambulance. He was wearing a uniform and an LAPD badge.

"Please," she said, fresh tears welling up. "You have to help the doctors believe me. My friend didn't overdose. I think someone sent me drugged or poisoned chocolates."

He looked her over and nodded slightly. "Let me help you out of there." The policeman steadied her as she climbed out. "I'm Detective Ostrich." He smiled grimly. "Yes, like the bird."

"Nice to meet you," Grace muttered. She was vaguely aware that life had handed her a gem at the very worst time.

"I came here because the EMTs say you're reporting this as a poisoning." The detective kept his face blank, but there was a dry tinge to his tone. He jerked his chin at the candy in her hands. "Is that the box of chocolates your friend was eating? May I see them?"

Grace nodded tightly, holding the box out to him, the contents rattling to the rhythm of her trembling. "They were for me. They came with this card." She handed it over.

Why would Nelson send her poisoned chocolates? Did his huggably-hairy exterior conceal a homicidal heart? She knew he was mad at her for that article, but he hadn't seemed *that* mad.

The detective snapped on latex gloves before taking the chocolates and card. He turned the card over in his hands, and rattled the chocolates around, examining the box. Then he called over a colleague, who stood with another cop by a pair of waiting cruisers, speaking with one of the EMTs.

"Get these analyzed," Detective Ostrich told the other cop. They stepped away a few paces and had a muttered conversation. Grace couldn't catch what they said, but they were shooting her little suspicious glances. She clenched her fists at her side and kept herself from barging over and knocking their heads together.

The other cop took the candy and went to one of the cruisers, speeding away with flashing lights. Detective Ostrich came back, looking her over again with the expression of judgment worn by every detective in the world, whether they live in L.A. or in a tiny cluster of shacks in the wide, forgotten tundra above the Arctic Circle. "We're just trying to figure out what's going on here," he said. "The medics said your friend shows signs of narcotics overdose."

"Zeus doesn't do narcotics," Grace spat. She remembered the Adderall, the weed, and the acid, but she'd been hiding and doling out his pills to him since the day he'd taken too many. Besides, she wasn't even sure weed or LSD were technically narcotics, and an overdose on those would just make Zeus extra Zeusy, not dead.

She squared her shoulders and took a deep breath so she wouldn't hiss like an angry cat. "Zeus has his share of problems, but narcotics aren't one. He doesn't have the money or the opportunity to get them even if he wanted. He doesn't so much as drink. If he has drugs in his system, then they were in the chocolates."

The detective nodded and hooked his thumbs in his utility belt. "This Zeus kid your boyfriend?"

Grace's eyes narrowed. "No. He's my foster son. He wasn't ready to be on his own when he turned eighteen." Her cheeks burned with indignation at his assumption.

The cop's eyebrows crept up. "What were you doing in that motel? That neighborhood's not much of a vacation spot."

Grace dug her fingernails into her palms. The man was named after a zoo animal, and she wasn't going to be intimidated. "We've been living there while I try to find steadier work. I'm a freelance journalist." She saw a smirk grow behind the cop's deliberately blank expression. She was tired of that smirk, which she always got when she told people about her situation. She stomped. "Please. I just need to know if Zeus is okay, and I need to figure out what's really going on here. If those chocolates were poisoned—"

"We're having them analyzed. If they're poisoned, our tests will show that."

"How long will the tests take? How are the doctors going to treat him if they can't even figure out what's making him sick?"

"The doctors here know what they're doing. They'll figure out what's making him sick in a jiffy and take good care of him. He'll be fine."

Grace glared at him through a fresh wave of tears, wondering if he'd offer her a lollipop next, tell her to run along and play and not worry her little head. She got some small satisfaction when he looked away and rubbed his nose.

"Look," he said. "Let's go inside and see how your friend is doing."

"Could you at least call and make sure they test those chocolates right away?"

"Ma'am, I assure you they'll test the chocolates immediately, but the hospital will test your friend's blood and figure out what's making him sick sooner than we can.

Come on, let's go inside, okay?"

Grace took a deep breath and nodded curtly. They turned and walked through the automatic doors into the waiting room.

Detective Ostrich gestured toward some empty chairs in the corner. "Why don't you go have a seat over there? I'm going to talk to the nurse and make sure they keep us up to date on your friend's condition."

"Thank you," Grace said.

She waded through the bad-smelling and noisy crowd. This definitely wasn't Cedars Sinai. Tired moms slumped in their seats as children wailed and scampered around them; haggard-faced old alcoholics drooped over their knees; perfectly-made-up young women clutched imitation designer handbags, looking as if their only emergency was they'd run out of diet pills. Grace fought back a wave of anguish. She'd trade places with *any* of these people rather than face the prospect of losing Zeus.

He'll be okay. They revived him. They know how to deal with this sort of thing in an L.A. hospital, the capital of drug overdoses. But she was just giving herself the same condescending speech that Ostrich had.

She sank into the cleanest seat in the corner, free of ketchup smears or crumpled candy wrappers. A bony woman three seats down glanced at her suspiciously, then went back to her current occupation of coughing wetly into a wadded-up napkin.

Grace felt a buzzing in her pocket and pulled out her phone. When she saw the message, bile rose into her throat. It was from Nicole's number. She'd completely forgotten about Nicole.

Hey. Are you even coming?

She gritted her teeth against a wave of indignant irritation and made herself calm down. Nicole had no way of knowing what had happened to Zeus…hopefully.

As soon as her irritation dissipated, she felt bad. She'd begged for an interview, then stood her up.

I'm so sorry, Grace texted back. *Right after I hung up with you, Zeus collapsed. I'm at the ER right now. I completely forgot about our meeting because I was so scared.*

She sent the message, hardly caring if Nicole believed her. Her whole career could go up in flames right now as long as Zeus survived.

However, it was only a couple seconds before she got a reply.

OMG. Is he okay? What happened?

Grace wiped her eyes. *His heart stopped, but they revived him. They're working on him now, but I don't know how he is yet. I have no idea what happened. They're trying to figure that out.* There was no way she'd tell Nicole about the chocolates. Not until she figured out what was going on, anyway.

What ER are you at? Nicole asked, and Grace told her, wondering if she was actually going to come down. She'd appreciate the company, even of near-strangers.

Then she remembered something and opened a new text. *Zeus won't be at practice today*, she texted Lyssa. *He's in the hospital.*

She got an immediate, terrified-sounding response from the songwriter, and had to tell the story all over again. By the tone of Lyssa's messages, Grace was more certain than ever that she had a crush on Zeus—perhaps a more serious one than Grace had suspected. Lyssa said she was going to cancel practice and be at the hospital as soon as she could.

Grace's heart warmed; it was nice that Zeus had people to care about him besides her. Most people considered him a freak or a moron and wouldn't give him the time of day, something that hurt Zeus deeply and made Grace want to breathe fire. He'd finally found some true friends in what might be the most unlikely of places: L.A.'s shallow, money-driven music scene.

Grace pocketed her phone as Detective Ostrich sat down next to her, his elaborate uniform creaking. "The nurse will find us when they know something about your friend."

"Thank you," Grace said.

He squinted at her. "Who sent you the chocolates? The card said Nelson. Is *he* your boyfriend?"

Grace swallowed. "Nelson isn't…no. We had a couple of dates, but then had a falling-out because of something I put in an article about the frontwoman from his band."

She studied the detective's clean-cut cop face, wondering if he even listened to music. "Nelson is the drummer in a band called Karma Korn," she said.

A look of incredulous realization stole across Detective Ostrich's face, and for a moment his cop exterior melted and she saw the man behind the mask. "*You're* the woman that wrote that article everyone's mad about?"

A wave of nausea claimed her. "You've heard about that?"

He chuckled a bit dorkily. "Yeah, I've heard about it. What, do I live in a cave? They mentioned it on Fox News."

Grace suddenly felt like someone had poured concrete over her heart. "They mentioned it on *Fox News*?"

"You didn't know?"

Grace shook her head weakly. "I don't watch TV much, and I've been staying off the internet." Detective Ostrich chuckled, his bright blue eyes examining her with a different kind of interest. Grace sat up and rubbed her sore eyes. "It'd be weird for Nelson to send poisoned chocolates in his own name, right?"

The cop nodded. "That'd be pretty idiotic. But believe me, ma'am, I see plenty of idiocy in the world."

"I don't doubt it. But Nelson doesn't seem like that kind of idiot." She knew she was trying to convince herself as much as Ostrich. She wasn't desperate enough to date murderers, was she? Maybe her instincts had gotten clouded.

She massaged her temples. She had enough on her mind without worrying about her dating habits.

"There's someone else you should check out with regard to this," she said. "He's someone that was really mad about that article I wrote, and he keeps showing up everywhere, like he's been stalking Zeus and me, or Inez. His name is Gary."

Even though it seemed like sort of a long shot, Grace told the detective about their encounters with the little man and was gratified to see a spark of interest in his eyes. She gave him Gary's contact information, and he punched it all into his phone.

"I'll have them run a background check on him, and maybe we'll have another chat with the guy," Ostrich said.

Grace nodded. "Thank you."

She wondered whether Gary would be mad or excited to be the subject of a police investigation.

They sat in silence for a while. The detective tapped his shiny black shoes on the floor, watching the waiting room crowd with the aura of a cat in a room full of birds. People avoided his gaze as if afraid the cop would see evidence of their every crime in their eyes.

Grace's worries turned every minute into ten. It seemed like she was about to crumble into dust with age when a young woman in green scrubs entered the waiting room and made a beeline for them. Grace dried her tears, her heartbeat accelerating.

"Are you Grace Morgan?" the woman asked.

Grace clutched her knees. "Yes."

"I'm doctor Zuniga. I helped treat Zeus Mahoney."

The past tense in that sentence hit Grace like a meteor. "How is he?" she choked out.

"He's stable now, but resting."

Grace expelled a breath and hid her face in her shaking hands for a moment. "Oh, my God. Thank God. Thank you."

Detective Ostrich blew out a puff of air. "Did you figure out what he'd overdosed on?"

The doctor nodded. "We did a toxicology screen. Looks like flunitrazepam."

Grace's brow furrowed, but the detective's eyebrows shot up. "Roofies?"

Doctor Zuniga nodded again. "We pumped his stomach and gave him charcoal and romazicon, which is the antidote. He's going to be fine, but he must have had at least three milligrams of the stuff. That's a lot."

Grace stared at the doctor. Now that her worry was diminishing, rage had space to stretch out. "Who the fuck would do that? He could have died." Her teeth clenched. Would Nelson do that to Zeus, to her? Would Gary? The doctor and the cop were watching her, and she could barely get a breath.

"Well, Ms. Morgan, it looks like they were gunning for you if the drugs were in the chocolates," Detective Ostrich said. "I'd like to talk to this Nelson guy whose name was on the box. Do you have his number?"

Grace squeezed her eyes shut. "Yeah, I have it. I mean, I really don't think he did it…"

"I'd still like to speak to him."

Grace nodded tightly and pulled her phone from her pocket, scrolling through her contacts. She'd wanted to delete Nelson's number but hadn't been able to muster the determination. Now, she was probably subjecting him to this flightless bird of a cop for no good reason; she tried not to think of it as payback for him treating her like shit, but mostly she hoped it didn't piss him off worse. She was just complying with law enforcement orders, right?

After giving Ostrich the information Grace got to her feet and faced the doctor. "I want to see Zeus."

The doctor nodded. "He's in the recovery ward now, third floor, but I doubt he's awake yet."

"I want to be there when he wakes up," Grace said. "Zeus is a little…odd, and he might get weird ideas if he's somewhere new without knowing how he got there."

"I'll come with you," Detective Ostrich said, standing. "I'd like to ask him some questions when he wakes up. Don't worry, I'll take it easy on him," he added, when he saw Grace and the doctor's glares. "He's no way in trouble. I just need all the answers I can get."

Grace imagined a groggy Zeus being questioned by the police and decided Detective Ostrich probably deserved the sort of answers he'd get. She shook the doctor's hand, thanked her, and headed for the elevators, the cop close at her heels.

13

They found Zeus lying pale and still in his hospital bed, an IV in his arm, monitors beeping all around him. A male nurse with a clipboard looked up when they came in.

"How is he doing?" Grace asked. She went to Zeus's bedside and took his limp, clammy hand. The detective retreated to the far corner.

"He's fine," the nurse said. "It's good you got him in so quickly. We were able to get most of the drug out of his stomach before it hit his bloodstream. He'll probably feel a little woozy when he wakes up, but he'll make a full recovery."

"Thank God," Grace said.

The nurse bustled out. Grace brushed the curls from Zeus's forehead. She had never seen him this quiet; he generally twitched and mumbled even in his sleep, but he was just lying there, all the animation gone from his face. *When I find out who did this to him, I'll chop them into hash.*

A familiar voice rang out in the hallway, and Grace's spine jolted with surprise.

"My hospital was much better. This place smells like they keep cattle in the storerooms."

Inez appeared in the doorway. Her hair, now bright turquoise, was twined into Princess Leia buns. Nelson appeared at her side. When his eyes found Grace's, a complicated flood of emotions passed between them. She saw worry in his expression, and perhaps a bit of remorse, but no guilt. He was wearing a Calexico t-shirt tight enough to show his drummer muscles, and Grace had to fight an urge to rip it off him and run her hands over those pecs. *You're mad at him, remember?* Not to mention she was at her best friend's sickbed.

"We got here as quick as we could," Nelson said. "Is he okay?"

Grace's heart skittered at the gentleness in his tone. "They say he'll be fine. Did Nicole tell you he was here?"

Nelson nodded.

"She texted me about it as soon as you told her," Inez said. "She's down getting me a latte right now, then she'll be here, too." She came to Zeus's bedside, an uncharacteristically helpless look taking over her face as she took his other hand. "What happened to him?"

"He collapsed after eating chocolates."

"Chocolates?" Nelson said. "Is he allergic?" Grace watched him closely as he came to her side, gazing down at Zeus with a furrowed brow.

"No, he's not allergic," she said.

Detective Ostrich emerged suddenly from his corner, making them all jump: even Grace had half-forgotten he was there. He stared at Inez with glassy eyes, picking nervously at a button on his pistol holster. "Hey…uh, you're Inez Carter,"

Inez backed off slightly. "And you're a cop."

"Detective Ostrich, Los Angeles Police Department." He puffed out his chest as he held out his hand to her.

Inez took it gingerly, as if it might explode, her wary expression relaxing somewhat. "Nice to meet you, Detective, uh, Ostrich." She giggled. "Oh, my God, that's the best name ever. We should get married. Inez *Ostrich*. It's like an evil French guy saying 'A nice ostrich'." She snorted like a rooting hog while the detective blushed furiously. Then Inez's eyes fell back to Zeus's unconscious face, and her smile faded. Her gaze darted questioningly to Grace's. "Why are the cops here?"

Grace gathered her hands into fists. "Because someone sent me a box of chocolates heavily laced with roofies, and Zeus ate them. Detective Ostrich is investigating."

Inez scowled and cocked her head, and Nelson's lips twisted in confusion under his beard.

"Drugged chocolates?" Nelson said. "Are you serious?"

"Serious as a CPA convention. And the card they came with had your name on it, Nelson."

His face blanched and his mouth fell open. "Huh?"

Detective Ostrich roused himself, clearing his throat.

"Yes, and I'd like to ask you some questions about that."

Nelson gave the cop a panicked look. "I didn't send her any chocolates. I swear to God."

"Would you mind if we took a look at your credit card records?" Detective Ostrich asked.

Nelson stood stiffly, tugging at his beard, but he nodded. "I guess so. Whatever I have to do in order to stop you chasing false leads while you figure out what the hell is going on here."

Inez stood with her lips elaborately pursed in thought. "Why is everyone, like, getting drugged and stuff? Is this an episode of Scooby Doo? Is there some murderous g-g-ghost out there?"

"That's a good question," Grace muttered.

Detective Ostrich's puffed-out chest deflated. "What do you mean, everyone keeps getting drugged? Was there someone else?"

"Yeah, like, *me,*" Inez said. "I apparently overdosed on heroin even though that shit is natty and I didn't even take it."

"You mean, that wasn't an intentional overdose?" he asked. "That's what I heard reported in the media."

Inez blew a long raspberry, which petered out with a wet squeak. "*That's* what you heard reported in the media. I didn't take any drugs, at all. Zip, zero, zilch. Just saying 'no' is where it's at."

Grace was proud of Inez for keeping a straight face.

The cop shifted on his feet. "I need to make some calls. You," he jerked his chin at Nelson, "please stick around so we can talk later."

Nelson nodded.

Detective Ostrich strode out of the room. They all watched after him. "I think he finally believed me about the chocolates," Grace said. "I think before he thought it was just a regular overdose and that I was lying or in denial."

Nelson frowned deeply. "What the hell is going on here? This is *nuts*."

"I know," Inez said. "If people are gonna give us free drugs without us knowing it, they should give us *good* drugs. Not the killy kind."

Nelson passed his hand over his face. Then he looked at Grace, his eyes wide and earnest. "I didn't send those chocolates, Grace. I swear to God."

She gazed at him a long while, then nodded. "I know. Even you aren't that stupidly homicidal."

He squinted at her, shaking his head.

Zeus twitched. "Watch out for the robots," he muttered. "They have pure wasabi running through their veins."

"Zeus," Grace breathed.

"They'll roll all your best ideas into imaginary sushi. Faulty programming."

Nelson crowded closer to the bed, at Grace's side.

Zeus's eyes cracked open, slowly coming into focus. He winced weakly. "Gracie, I never want to eat sushi again.

That stuff is sickening." He glanced around. His eyes opened wider and his body went rigid. "Where are we? Is this the robots' spaceship? Am I being probed?"

"No, Zuzu," Grace said. "You're in the hospital. There aren't any robots, don't worry."

"There were robots, Gracie. How dare you say there were no robots?"

"Shhh, Zuzu. Really, there are no robots, and you didn't eat any sushi. You ate drugged chocolates."

He studied her face, then relaxed slightly. "Drugged chocolates? Cool. Did I have fun? Because I can't remember that." His gaze fell on Inez and he smiled hazily. "I must have had fun if Inez was there."

"Hi, Zeus." Inez kissed two of her fingers and placed them on his nose. "But you didn't have fun, though. Someone tried to kill you, like they did me."

"They did?" Zeus stiffened again. "I thought there were no robots, Gracie! Wasn't it the robots that were trying to kill me?"

"We don't know yet," Inez said. "Maybe. That'd be cool if it was. I'd probably make the cover of Rolling Stone if robots were trying to kill me."

"You already made the cover of Rolling Stone," Nelson said.

"Oh yeah, that's right. But still. I'd probably make it again."

"Were the robots trying to kill me in order to get my stoney chocolates?" Zeus asked. "And do I have any left? I could use a pick-me-up."

Grace and Nelson exchanged a long-suffering look.

There were footsteps on the hospital floor and Detective Ostrich came back into the room. Grace noticed a subtle difference in the way he regarded her, and a slight sheepish twist to his mouth.

"The initial analysis of those chocolates is back," he said. "They did indeed contain benzodiazapines—roofies. So it looks like that's how the drugs got into the young man's system." He noticed Zeus looking up at him and gave a small smile of surprise. "Oh, you're awake. Hello, Mr. Mahoney. My name is Detective Ostrich, with the Los Angeles Police Department. How are you feeling?"

Zeus went very still, gazing fixedly at the detective. "Gracie," he muttered out of the corner of his mouth. "The cops are here. The cops want to know how I'm feeling. What do I tell them, Gracie?"

An appraising look passed across the detective's face, and he shot Grace the is-this-guy-for-real glance. Grace was used to getting that look and tried to keep her eyes from rolling. "You could start by telling him how you feel, Zeus. It's okay to talk to him."

Zeus studied Detective Ostrich a few moments longer. "I feel very law-abiding. I haven't always felt that way, but I do now. You can put that in my file. Also, do you know my father, Sergeant Jared Ingrams with the Seattle Police Department? I'm sure he would be very upset about the sushi space robots trying to murder his son, as well as Inez, who is a very important internationally famous rock star. I'm positive he would tell you to open an investigation of the matter."

The cop opened his mouth, closed it, and looked at Grace for a translation. She was also used to people asking her for translations, but she didn't want to play that game. The detective seemed to sense this from her glare and turned back to Zeus, clearing his throat.

"I *am* doing an investigation, in fact. Do you mind if I ask you some questions? Are you feeling up to it?"

"Up to it and down for it," Zeus said. Then the IV in his left arm caught his attention, and he sat up slightly, examining it. "I'm plugged in. Am I electrical now? What sort of mechanical engineering did those robots do?" He tugged at the line, and Grace caught his hand.

"Don't pull it, Zeus. It's an IV."

He stopped tugging. Grace stared at him pointedly, giving him her best it's-time-to-act-normal look. He gazed back at her, then settled back against his pillows primly. "Okay, officer, I'm ready to answer your questions now."

"Thank you," Detective Ostrich said. "First of all, could you tell me what happened before you lost consciousness?"

Zeus' eyes hazed over. He fiddled distractedly with the line of his IV. "We were in our motel room. Gracie had gone to the store to get lettuce because we were going to party with some rabbits, and I was doing my upper body workout routine."

Detective Ostrich glanced at Grace again; she crossed her arms and kept her eyes on Zeus.

Zeus's brow furrowed. "Was there some guy that came to the door? It makes my brain squirm around to think about it." He gazed distantly at the wall, rubbing his temples. "Some guy came to the door. Some monkey in a suit, bearing gifts. Maybe he was a sushi space robot monkey. But that's all I remember."

"That's weird," Inez said. "The last thing I remember was someone coming to the door, too."

"Were you expecting a package from Nelson that day?" Grace asked. Nelson sighed and pinched the bridge of his nose. "Just joking," Grace said.

"It was the robot space monkeys at the door both times," Zeus said. "That's probably their MO. They open the door, and light shines out of it all trippy like on *2001: Space Odyssey*. And it wipes your memory."

"Weird," Inez said.

Detective Ostrich looked between Zeus and Inez, then seemed to rouse himself. "Yeah, well, it's not uncommon for victims of overdose to have amnesia about events that occurred before they lose consciousness. Sometimes the memories return, though there's debate about whether those are true memories, or implanted ones. The mind tries to piece together what happened by inserting scenes based on what other people say happened."

Grace was impressed by this show of intellect, but Ostrich looked a little embarrassed, giving an uncomfortable shrug.

"Anyway," he said, "that's what I've heard. The doctors will know more about it." He turned his attention back to Zeus, who had gone pale again.

"I don't feel shipshape," he said. "I don't feel any sort of shape at all, in fact. I feel like a big blorb. Very pudding-like." He wrinkled his nose. "Pudding sounds gross."

The detective nodded resignedly. He fished in one of his many pockets and brought out business cards, handing them to Grace and Inez. "Call me if anybody remembers anything else, will you?"

"Of course," Grace said. "But you're not leaving the investigation at that, are you?"

"No. In fact, I'd still like to chat with Nelson over here. Right now, if he has the time." He nodded in his direction. "We'll follow a few other leads as well. That other individual you mentioned, we'll look him up. And we'll call the shop that delivered the flowers and candy."

"Thank you," Grace said. "You'll let me know, right?"

The detective nodded. His eyes flicked over to Zeus, whose eyelids were fluttering closed. For a moment, Grace saw the human being behind the cop again. He smiled and patted her on the shoulder. "I'm glad he's okay. He seems like a good kid, and he's lucky to have you looking after him."

Grace nodded, smiling slightly. People always said that, but they never realized *she* was also lucky to have Zeus looking after *her*.

The detective turned to Nelson. "We could talk in the waiting room."

Nelson nodded unhappily. "Uh, sure. Why not."

The two of them went out, scooting around Nicole as she came through the doorway carrying a cardboard tray of coffees. Grace saw Ostrich glance back as he left, eyeing the DJ's bright orange leggings and beaded fringe skirt. Nicole glanced after him in turn.

"What's with the cops?" she murmured as she came in. She handed Inez a coffee and received a wet smooch on the cheek as payment. She passed a cup to Grace as well. "Thought you might need this."

Grace smiled. "That's incredibly sweet of you. And thank you for coming, especially after I stood you up like that."

"Under the circumstances, it's completely understandable. What happened, anyway?"

Grace pressed her lips together. "Someone sent me roofied chocolates. Zeus ate them and overdosed."

"*What?*" Nicole said. "That's crazy!"

"And that's not the nutsiest thing," Inez said. "The card they came with had Nelson's name on it."

Nicole's mouth fell open.

"I *know*, right?" Inez said. "Everyone is getting drugged around here. It's like a frat party."

Nicole frowned, playing with the stir stick poking from the lid of her coffee cup. "You don't really think Nelson did it, do you, Grace? Because Nelson wouldn't."

"Totally," Inez said. "He wouldn't even have the drugs to do it with. He's such a nerd about those things. *Inez, don't drink so much. Inez, you shouldn't take cough syrup recreationally. Inez, PCP won't make your songwriting any better.* Blah, blah, blah."

Nicole's face filled with frustration as she gazed at her girlfriend. Grace wondered why a woman who seemed so together would be in love with a hot philandering mess like Inez. But she guessed Inez had her fine points, and everyone had their weaknesses.

"No, I definitely don't think Nelson did it," Grace said. "I don't think the cops think so, either. They're just checking up."

"But who *would* do it?" Nicole mused. "Who has it out for both you and Inez? Because the two druggings have to be related, right?"

Zeus twitched in his sleep, muttering something about chickens laying scrambled eggs. Grace sipped her coffee, feeling its heat settle into her bones. "I don't have the slightest idea. If the person who poisoned Inez is really someone who is mad at Inez about…you know…what I said in my article," she winced as Nicole's face clouded with hurt, "it really doesn't make sense that they'd go after me, too. I mean, why would they be mad at Inez and me both? It's contradictory. And also, if it was just some random fan or crazy person, how would they have known to send the card with Nelson's name on it?"

Nicole and Inez stared at her. "What, you didn't hear?" Inez asked.

Grace's hand tightened on the coffee cup. "Hear what?"

Inez giggled. "Oh, my God, I thought for sure you would have read it. That other reporter chick, you know, the one who wrote that bullshit *We Love Inez the Lez* article, wrote another one about you and Nelson. 'Reporter who defamed Inez Carter dating Karma Korn's drummer,' or whatever. She tried to insinuate you were using Nelson for story fodder, to gain some sort of insider status to further your career. Nelson was so embarrassed and angry about it. At the other chick, not you," she added.

"Marla Poccino wrote another article?" Grace whipped out her phone and searched Google. "And Nelson was mad about it? So, you mean…it's not Nelson giving Marla information?"

Inez scrunched up her face as if Grace had offered her a fried slug sandwich. "What? No way. Nelson wouldn't talk to that hog twat. I don't know where she's getting her information, but it's not from him. After Nelson read her stupid article that said I tried to kill myself like some tweeny drama queen, I think he felt bad about getting mad at you for what you wrote. I mean, at least you were telling the truth, and you weren't *trying* to stir up shit." She twirled a lock of hair around her finger, giving Grace a half-smile. "He really likes you, you know."

Grace's cheeks burned. "I, uh…" She rubbed her nose, her hand muffling the "reallylikehimtoo." She straightened her shoulders, avoiding the gossipy smirks of the other two women. "But, all of this sort of raises more questions."

Grace turned her attention back to her phone and found the article they were talking about, again on the *Celebrity Life* website. Her face reached the approximate temperature of a glass kiln as she scanned it. "That little snatchmuffin!"

Inez laughed. "For real. That Marla chick is totally baking up some muffins with that snatch."

Grace huffed and tossed her phone into her purse, worried she'd crush it between her fingers if she continued to hold it. "Why won't that freckled biddy stay out of my business? What is she doing this for? *She's* the one using insider information to further her career and spread lies." Grace took several deep breaths, trying to suppress the desire to strip Marla Poccino naked, cover her in bacon grease, tie her to a palm along Sunset Boulevard, and release a box full of wasps on her. The tourists would snap photos while she was stung to mush.

It wasn't fair that Marla was so successful when Grace was struggling. Were lies and a willingness to hurt people what it took to get ahead as a freelance journalist? And where the *hell* was Marla getting her inside info, anyway, if it wasn't Nelson?

Grace's anger deflated when she focused on Nicole, who was staring forlornly at her coffee cup. "I guess that article is no more than I deserve, after all the trouble I've caused you guys," Grace said.

Nicole looked up and tried to smile. "You're not causing me any trouble."

"You didn't cause me any trouble, either," Inez said. "If some crazy person is trying to kill me because of that article you wrote, that's not really your fault. And I'm fine, so no harm done."

Grace chewed her cheek, frowning at Zeus's inert form. Had her article caused this attack, as well? She couldn't think of any other reason someone would send her poisoned chocolates. But why would someone be so pissed off at her for saying Inez was bisexual, but also pissed off at Inez because she might not be? None of that made sense. There were either two separate killers with a similar MO, or she was missing the motive here.

All this rambled around in her mind, but she pushed it out. There was another, much simpler mystery that she had to solve if she wanted to keep herself in ramen and Zeus in psych meds.

But would it put them in even more danger if she published a follow-up article on Inez's love life?

Grace tried to fend off a headache. The killer or killers would likely strike again, no matter what she did; she could think of no reason why they'd attempt murder twice, fail both times, and then lose interest. Perhaps, if she published another article, it would ferret them out and reveal their motive. The thought made her shudder. *I'll just have to be careful. I'll throw all candy deliveries away immediately and tell Nelson to keep a closer eye on Inez.*

Grace licked her dry lips, feeling like a doofus as she fumbled around for a segue. She smiled grimly at Inez. "Marla had every right to write that article accusing me of defamation, though, if I somehow misinterpreted something between you and Zeus."

Nicole looked like she wanted to flutter off to perch on a power line, far above this conversation. Inez put her hand on her shoulder, but Nicole shrugged it off. "I've gotta go to the bathroom," Nicole muttered.

Inez watched sadly as her girlfriend stalked out. "You didn't misinterpret anything," Inez said. "What can I say? Zeus is just mega awesome." She gently pressed a turquoise fingernail to Zeus's nose. "Boop." He stirred and muttered something about a time-delay button.

Grace glanced out the open door where Nicole had gone. "I hurt Nicole with what I wrote, though, and I feel bad about that."

"She'll get over it. She knows I don't want a serious relationship right now. I've talked to her about it." Inez shuffled her feet, looking uncharacteristically self-conscious.

Grace resolved to have a talk with Zeus about Inez when he woke up, because Grace would be damned if the singer played him like she was playing Nicole. "I mean, not to get technical or anything," Grace said, "but if you like Zeus, then you're not really a lesbian, right?"

Inez's brow furrowed. "I've always liked some dudes, just not that often. I've mostly called myself a lesbian because it's easier than dealing with the fallout of saying you're bi or pan. You know, the people who say you're not queer enough, that you need to 'decide on a side,' or the sort of men who approach you looking for orgies."

Grace snorted. "I get that, yeah. But what about all that crap you said about the only thing you hate more than sex with men is—"

"—is 'the bigot racist dipshit Nazis in congress, and people who fart on airplanes.'" Inez laughed. "Duke wrote that line, or one of his minions did, probably, because he isn't that funny. Duke told me to say it, and I did, because it's hilarious."

"*Duke* told you to say that?"

Inez patted her hair buns. "I know, weird right? But whatever."

Grace chewed her lip. *I still have a lot to learn about L.A.'s depravity, apparently.* "Inez, would you be willing to do an interview with me talking about some of this stuff? Maybe clearing up the sexual orientation thing?"

Inez studied her, a corner of her silver-painted lips curling up. "You just want to get back at that other reporter chick who keeps writing those articles about you, right?"

"Yeah. And save my career, because everyone thinks I'm a liar." Grace swirled her coffee in its paper cup, frowning. "*High Note* gave me five days to write a follow-up article about you before they print a retraction, saying I was mistaken about you not being a lesbian. Apparently they can't handle the controversy."

Inez clicked her tongue a few times and shrugged. "That really sucks. Especially since you were only telling the truth in the first place." She grinned. "Okay. I'll give you the real scoop on what I do with my vuh-jay-jay, if you want."

Grace expelled a breath. "Thank you."

Inez blew a raspberry. "I'm tired of Duke's, um, hard line on the matter, anyway. My hoo-hah isn't a brand or a commodity. It is what it is, and it's time the world had the hot, wet truth." She stomped her combat boot, and Grace couldn't help but giggle.

They sat at Zeus's bedside, Grace's phone recorder running as she asked Inez a series of questions about her sexuality and romantic life. Nicole wandered in with a glum expression just as Grace asked whether Inez ever saw herself getting married.

Inez grinned as Nicole plopped forlornly into the adjacent chair. "I don't know," Inez said with a wistful note in her voice. "I figure I'll get married someday, but right now I think I'm too immature or something. I wouldn't make a good wife, because I'm still at the point where I want to screw everyone I meet who's hot and cool. Eventually I'm sure I'll calm down about it, because sex isn't everything, and finding that one person that you can truly call yours, that always has your back, is the most important thing." She took Nicole's hand, and the other woman gave her a tentative smile.

Zeus twitched in his sleep, muttering, "We need some more shoe polish for our enemies, Gracie."

A voice spoke from the doorway. "Well, honesty is the best policy, I guess."

Nelson held Grace's gaze as he came in and sat next to her. He reached out and tentatively interlocked his fingers with hers. "I'm sorry I was a jerk to you."

She stared breathlessly into those blue eyes. "It's okay. I shouldn't have written that article without talking to you guys, anyway."

Grace decided she was probably the worst journalist on the planet, but maybe that spoke in her favor.

Footsteps sounded in the hallway, and they all glanced up. In came Lyssa Medlin, her swinging ponytails at odds with her worried look. "Hey, y'all." She clasped a huge stuffed teddy bear in her arms. It wore a leather jacket, a plush cigarette dangled from its lips, and its round belly had "METAL!" embroidered on it in jagged letters. A bouquet of balloons plunked together above, their strings tied to the bear's fuzzy wrist.

The smile of greeting Lyssa gave Inez suggested a hope that Inez would be laid low by a raging case of hemorrhoids. Then her gaze slid to Zeus's slack face, and her expression reverted to worry. She set the bear down on the table took his hand.

Inez gave a small, derisive snort.

Zeus stirred. "Look both ways, Gracie," he mumbled.

Lyssa looked close to tears. "Is he going to be all right?"

"He'll be fine," Grace said. "He was awake not long ago, but he's still sleeping off the drugs I guess."

"Tell me the whole story," Lyssa said. "Someone sent you drugged chocolates? That's so…British murder mystery-esque."

"Tell me about it." Grace said. She launched into the story again, Lyssa's eyes going wider as she listened.

"So, wait," Lyssa said, her gaze darting to Nelson.

"Wasn't me," Nelson said tiredly. "I was in the library with a candlestick at the time."

Lyssa's brow furrowed. "But who could have done it?"

"The same person who poisoned me, probably," Inez said, crossing her legs and looking anywhere but at Lyssa.

Lyssa cocked her hip slightly and raised an eyebrow. "What do you mean? Didn't you just overdose on smack?"

Inez's lip curled. "I'll overdose on smacking you."

Nicole, who was sitting between them, looked like she'd

rather be scrubbing public toilets. Nelson exchanged a half-panicked look with Grace. "Now, girls, this is a hospital room," he said. "Try not to get in slap fights."

Lyssa looked sheepish, but Inez said something surly under her breath.

"I don't get it," Lyssa said. "Who would have it out for both Inez and Grace?"

"I figure it must have something to do with that article I wrote about Zeus that mentioned Inez," Grace said. She rubbed the tense muscles in her neck, craving a shot of whiskey to dull the sharp edges of this day.

Nelson squeezed her hand and gave her a reassuring smile, and Grace smiled back, deciding Nelson was worth at least three shots of whiskey.

Zeus stirred. His eyes opened, and he blinked at Lyssa. "Hey," he said sleepily.

Lyssa's face lit up. "Hey. How are you feeling?"

"I don't think I'm going to make it to practice today," Zeus said. "I'm really sorry."

Lyssa giggled, smoothing the curls from his forehead. "Don't worry about that, Zeus. I canceled practice. Just get better." She continued to hold his hand, and Zeus gazed up at her with big eyes, looking shy and somewhat baffled. Inez and Nicole continued their respective sulking.

Despite how tiresome it was, Grace was a little bit proud that Zeus had inadvertently caused so much drama among this elite group of international rock stars.

The doctors agreed Zeus was stable but recommended he be kept another night for observation. As Grace drove back to the motel later that evening, the phone with her precious tabloid interview safely in her purse, she wondered whether being a journalist wasn't really her calling. She'd done well enough covering the Seattle music scene. That had involved mostly hanging out with friends and going to shows. Asking hard-hitting questions, however—being nosy, and prying into people's personal business—wasn't comfortable for her. Friendship was more important than her career, a sentiment that had now kept her from breaking several sensational stories.

Marla Pocchino didn't seem to have the same qualms, unfortunately.

Grace consoled herself that her gentler methods had paid off this time, though. An exclusive, personal, and in-depth interview with Inez Carter about her sexual orientation was pure pop-culture gold right now. She'd recover her reputation and then some, and would be drinking brand-name soda in her own apartment in no time. Maybe, just maybe, she'd be able to build a career on the article and get future stories without stepping on so many toes.

All she had to do was type the thing up and get it to Lawrence.

The motel room was strange and lonely. Without Zeus's

constant chatter, or the television blasting reality shows while he did his workout, Grace could hear the guests in the adjacent rooms. On one side, a couple was arguing heatedly in Spanish; on the other, a woman was moaning and crying out theatrically, accompanied by the rhythmic thumping of the headboard. Grace hoped the woman was having as much fun as she was letting on.

Grace sighed and popped in earplugs before sitting back on her bed, opening her laptop and starting in on the article.

It took her a moment to realize that the muffled buzz wasn't her neighbors' antics; it was her cell ringing on the pressboard nightstand. She almost missed the call.

It was a local number she didn't recognize. She jabbed the answer button and wrestled one of her earplugs out. "Hello?"

"Ms. Morgan?" A female voice, polite but worried.

"This is she."

"Hi. My name is Carla Clinton, and I'm calling from the hospital."

Grace's heart threatened to jump out of her throat. "Is Zeus okay? What happened?"

There was a pause, and Grace had to struggle to breathe. "That's what we're concerned about," Carla said. "I take it he's not with you?"

"*Shit,*" Grace spat. "He's gone? He left?"

"I'm afraid he's missing from his room. He hasn't been

discharged yet. We thought there might have been a mix-up, that he might have left with you."

"No, he's not with me. Shitshitshit." *How could I have taken off and left him alone? He was all drugged up and didn't know what was happening.* She looked frantically around the room, as if he might be there and she just forgot.

"We'll search the remainder of the hospital," Carla said, a note of panic edging its way into her voice. "You might want to call the police, though I don't know if they'll file a missing person report yet. Perhaps you can get them to if you mention he's…"

Special. "Sure, okay, thanks."

Grace hung up. She sprang out of bed, then stood there sweating and breathing hard as she wondered what to do next. She'd settled on driving over to the hospital and cruising the surrounding streets, and was grabbing her purse and keys, when her phone rang again.

A wave of mixed hope and dread washed through her as she fished her phone out of her purse, scattering tissues and tubes of lipstick. Unknown number. She answered breathlessly. "Hello?"

After a slight pause, Stephen Hawking's computer voice started speaking, but it didn't have anything to say about astrophysics. "We have your friend Zeus," it said flatly. "At midnight tonight, you will leave your laptop computer in the dumpster behind Sally's Kitchen on East Fourth Street. After you do so, you will receive a call with further instructions. You will delete all audio files from your cell phone. You will not attempt to publish any more articles about celebrities or the music scene. We will know immediately if you don't follow any of these instructions. We will know if you are trying to track or follow us. We will know if you contact the police. If you don't follow our instructions, we will kill you, and your friend."

The line clicked and beeped as the call disconnected. Grace stood shaking, the phone still pressed to her sweaty ear.

14

Grace watched the red numbers on the cheap alarm clock turn over, her mind filled with images of a confused and groggy Zeus tied to a chair in some stranger's basement. Once the drugs from the chocolates wore off fully, he'd be hopping around on the chair singing Tool songs. They'd probably beat him unconscious to save themselves the annoyance. *Don't think about that.*

Who were his captors? What were they trying to accomplish? Grace couldn't organize her thoughts. The kidnapping and both druggings had to be related somehow, and they all were related to her articles, but the connection seemed too tenuous, and the subject of her articles too petty, to warrant all these felonies.

She covered her face with her hands, breathing through her fingers as she rolled all she knew and all the potential culprits through her mind. If the person had access to all this information, that meant that, at some point, Grace had looked into the eyes of someone capable of kidnapping and attempted serial murder. She couldn't think of anyone who set off alarm bells of that timbre, but she'd been wrong about people before. After all, she hadn't figured out what a jerkwad her ex-husband was until it was too late.

Grace didn't want to start suspecting everyone she knew, but she had to figure this out soon. If whoever it was kept trying to murder people, they'd be successful at it sooner or later, because any crapbrain could achieve a lofty goal through persistence.

Grace had a feeling that even if she ditched her laptop in the dumpster, Zeus wouldn't be returned to her safe and sound. If she and Zeus were allowed to go free, the person or people behind this would have no way of keeping them from going to the police, or of assuring that Grace would never again write an article about anyone in the music scene. No—they'd wanted her and Inez dead before, and they weren't likely to settle for less than murder at this point.

Midnight was only five hours away. She took a deep breath and picked up her phone.

Then hesitated. The message said she wasn't to contact the police, but it didn't explicitly forbid her from contacting anyone else. They probably wouldn't be happy about it if they knew, though. How closely were they watching her?

Grace chewed her lip. The only reliable way to track her calls and texts would be by installing spyware on her phone. But she was one of those people who never left her phone behind, even for a split second. How would they have had time? It seemed more likely that the kidnapper or kidnappers were bluffing, and that they wouldn't immediately know what she was up to.

Even if they didn't know, though, was this the right thing? Could he be trusted?

Her heart said yes. Though she knew her heart to be both foolish and traitorous, she dialed the number.

**

She waited at the backmost table, stirring a tortilla chip in a dish of eyebrow-singeing pico de gallo. The taquería was on a quiet street about a mile from her motel, and the dining area was dark, narrow, and nearly deserted. If the perpetrator of this drama had enough resources to stalk her and deal with Zeus at the same time, at least she'd have a good chance of spotting them in the act, which was half the battle to begin with.

She might be endangering Zeus's life with this meeting, but she'd be endangering it, and her own, even more if she walked into this situation without any sort of backup. At least that's what she told herself. Otherwise, she'd second-guess what she was doing and worry about it until she exploded all over the orange-painted walls.

The bell over the door jingled, and Nelson strode in, slicking back his unruly red hair. He grinned when he saw her, but that grin faded as he slid into the plastic bench seat opposite her. "You look terrified. Is everything okay?"

Grace swallowed, her gaze darting around the room and out the front windows. There was only one other customer, an elderly man who was shouting at the televised soccer match in hoarse Spanish. The street outside was quiet.

"Zeus was kidnapped," she muttered.

Nelson's eyes went wide. "Are you fucking serious?" The other customer glanced back at them, but soon resumed his impassioned soccer commentary. Nelson dropped his voice lower. "Sorry."

Grace shrugged miserably. "It's okay. And yes, I'm serious."

Nelson blinked at her. The proprietor of the restaurant bustled up, grinning. He handed Nelson a menu and took his stuttered drink order of a Corona with lime before trotting off again. Nelson's eyes didn't leave Grace's face the whole time. "What the hell happened?"

Grace told him about the call from the hospital, then the one from the kidnappers, as all color left Nelson's face. The waiter brought his beer and Nelson took it distractedly, his knuckles going white around the bottle.

"What the fuck?" He stared at the table a long moment, tugging at his beard. "Who could be doing this?"

"I have no idea. But it has to be someone we both know, right? Who else would have access to all the information they'd need?"

"I don't know, but it's not necessarily someone we know. It could be someone who's just really good at internet stalking. Or maybe they have one of us bugged."

She pushed around chunks of tomato and pepper with her now-soggy chip. "Maybe, but I don't know how. Do you ever leave your phone lying around so that people could bug it?"

Nelson gave a dry laugh. "No, phonie and I are joined at the hip."

"Same. I really don't think I could be bugged, at least not that way." She shuddered. The thought of her phone betraying her was almost as bad as assuming it was one of her friends.

Nelson sent lime juice trickling into his sunshine-golden beer. The waiter came, and even though Grace wasn't the least bit hungry, she ordered two carnitas tacos out of habit. Nelson ordered a plate of churros and another beer, even though he hadn't even started on his first one. The waiter left, and Nelson leaned back in his bench seat. "I just can't think of who it could possibly be."

"Well, there is this one weird guy," Grace said, and told him about Gary.

Nelson's lips twisted in a reluctant smirk. "He sounds like some weird creeper fan, not someone with a huge vendetta."

"My gut tells me it's not him, but I can't be sure."

"Who else could it be, though?"

Grace's gaze fell to the table. She finally ate the chip, grimacing at its lack of crunch. "I don't know. It could be more than one person. You know, people with separate motives, one against me and the other against Inez. I can't think of many people who would have a grudge against both of us. Maybe Gary tried to off Inez, or maybe even…I mean, Lyssa Medlin…"

Nelson scoffed. "That sweet girl? I seriously doubt that. I mean, yeah, it doesn't seem like she's all about Inez and Zeus's little fling, but petty jealousy doesn't usually translate into homicide."

"Not in most circles, but this is L.A."

Nelson laughed between his teeth. "L.A people have better ways of getting back at their romantic rivals. Murder gets blood all over their Jimmy Choos."

Grace nodded halfheartedly. "I don't have any other ideas, though."

Nelson tapped his fingers on the table, lost in thought. Grace picked up another chip, resumed stirring, then flung the chip down on her napkin. "If I don't figure this out soon, they're going to hurt Zeus."

Nelson let out a huge breath, his shoulders sagging. Then he squared them and took Grace's hand in his. "We're going to figure this out, okay? He's going to be fine."

Grace nodded, her tears splattering the tabletop. She couldn't bring herself to believe a word of it.

He squeezed her hand. "Here's what I think we should do."

She glanced up at him; she was glad for that "we" almost as much as she was glad he had a plan, because right now she was lucky to have a thought, much less a plan of her own.

"First of all, I don't think you should call the police," Nelson said. "No matter how unlikely it is, your cell phone might be tracked, and you shouldn't risk Zeus' life like that. Whoever it is might be tracking my phone, too, so I don't think I should call them on my phone. But, I do think the police should be called."

"How?" Grace tried to keep the frustration out of her voice. She'd hoped his plan would be better than this. "And do you really think calling the cops would do any good, anyway? I'm sure the kidnapper would notice if I rolled up with Andy Griffith and Dirty Harry to drop off the laptop."

Nelson chuckled. "I think it will help to have the police involved even if they can't go with you to the drop. I'm going to a pay phone to call Detective Ostrich, because the kidnapping is almost certainly related to Zeus's poisoning, and probably Inez's as well. If they have any leads in those cases, maybe they can get to the bottom of this."

Grace chewed her cheek. She nodded. "Okay. I trust you to do whatever you think is right."

She realized that wasn't just lip service. How long had it been since she'd trusted someone that much? Probably never.

Nelson reached over and tucked one of her curls behind her ear with a drumstick-calloused thumb. "We're going to find Zeus. We're smarter than whoever this dipshit is."

She wiped her eyes, nodding. She wanted to believe him. Even if he was wrong, she was glad she was here. It would have been a lot harder to face all this alone. She checked the time on her phone. "It's already eight."

It seemed like this day had lasted two years, but the sun had just set.

"That will give the cops time to get things set up." Nelson downed the rest of his first beer just as the waiter brought him his new one and slid their plates of food in front of them.

Nelson stood as the waiter left. "I'm going to go call Detective Ostrich. I'll be right back. Just wait here, okay?"

"Okay." She hugged herself, not wanting him to leave even for a minute. She hated to admit it, but she felt safer with him there, like she was an aging damsel in distress and he a strong, hairy knight in cargo shorts. "Nelson? Be careful."

He smiled faintly. "I will. I'll keep an eye out for anyone tailing me, and I shouldn't take more than fifteen minutes, okay?" He jerked his chin at his plate. "Don't eat all my churros."

She snorted, then had to wipe her nose. "I won't."

15

The bell over the door jingled as Nelson left. The restaurant owner peeked out from the kitchen, raising his eyebrows at the scene of Grace crying alone with the two plates of food. He retreated quickly with an alarmed expression.

Grace nibbled at her tacos and watched through the front windows as the last of the day's light faded, leaving the streetlights to illuminate the cracked and trash-strewn pavement. A man with week-old-roadkill hair sat against the wall of a liquor store, goggling at the occasional passing car or pedestrian and rolling a cigarette. He was the only person in sight, and he didn't look like he had the stamina to involve himself in a murder and kidnapping plot. Besides, he probably would leave a stench as unique as a fingerprint at any crime scene and be easy to identify.

Soon, roadkill-hair was joined in his puddle of streetlight by a scrawny guy who scratched constantly at the front of his stained wifebeater.

Grace pulled apart her tacos until they looked like a

firecracker had gone off inside them, but still Nelson didn't reappear. She checked her phone with a trembling hand. It was eight thirty-five, and his fifteen minutes had been up fifteen minutes ago. The nervous restaurant owner peeked out of the kitchen at her again, perhaps wondering if he was going to have to let her cry on his shoulder about her relationship woes before she'd finally pay the check and leave.

The two guys across the street perked up as a Camaro cruised slowly by, causing small earthquakes with blasting bass. The two guys scampered after it like overgrown kids chasing a felonious ice cream truck. *They're definitely not here to spy on me.*

She checked her phone again. Eight forty-five. She pulled Nelson's number up on her phone, her thumb hesitating over the dial button. If their phones were being traced, she'd run a risk by calling him in the first place. How much worse would she make it by calling him again?

I can't make it much worse if Nelson is already dead or kidnapped, she thought with a shudder of panic. She pressed the dial button.

The bell over the restaurant's door dinged. Grace expelled a breath as Nelson strode in, pulling his ringing cellphone out of his pocket. He glanced at the screen and smirked at her, hitting the answer button. "Hello?"

She hung up, letting out a shuddering sigh of relief. Nelson replaced his phone in his pocket and slid into the seat next to Grace, pulling his plate toward him and taking a huge swig of his beer. "Sorry it took so long."

The restaurant owner peeked out of the kitchen again, a relieved grin spreading over his face before he pulled his head back in.

"What happened?" Grace asked.

Nelson wrinkled his nose and picked up a churro. "I had to try about six different payphones. They were all out of service."

"So, what happened?"

He crunched his pastry and swallowed. "My churros got cold for one thing." Grace gave him The Look, which apparently worked on him as well as Zeus because he looked abashed. "An officer is coming here to meet with us," he said. "Should be here any minute."

Grace's stomach clenched, and she was glad she hadn't eaten her poor tacos. "Isn't that too dangerous? Won't the kidnappers know?"

"Ostrich said whoever it is will be undercover. It's as safe as possible, and I think it's safer than sending you in to meet with these people without any police involvement."

Grace shredded a piece of tortilla into even smaller bits.

Nelson reached out to take her hand. "Stop mangling your poor food. And have a churro, you didn't eat anything, you just rearranged it." He held one out to her.

"I'm not hungry."

He waved it in her face. "Eat the churro before the churro eats you, Grace."

She rolled her eyes and took it from him, taking a bite. It was indeed cold, and her lack of appetite made her feel like she was eating Styrofoam peanuts, but it made her happy that Nelson was trying to take care of her.

Nelson regarded her with worry. He downed the rest of his beer and forced a grin. "Did you hear the one about the fire at the campground?"

Grace paused in her chewing. "No."

"It was in-tents." He drummed the table and flicked his beer bottle with his fingernails. *Buh-dump ting.*

Grace winced.

"Sorry," he said. "Maybe a funnier guy would be better at lightening the mood."

She slid her foot over until her thigh nestled alongside his. "Under the circumstances, I doubt it." He smiled in a way that made her cheeks go warm. "Nelson? Thank you. For being here, and for everything."

"I'm glad to be here. Just wish the circumstances were different."

The bell over the door tinkled, and a man in jeans and a t-shirt strutted in, somehow looking more like a cop than if he'd been in uniform. It was probably the way he'd tried to smooth his buzz cut with too much gel. The restaurant owner peeked out again and retreated like a gopher who had seen a hawk. Grace was glad she didn't need her water glass filled.

The cop came to their table and nodded in greeting. "You're Grace Morgan and Nelson Taylor?"

They both made affirmative noises. The man held his hand out to Grace. "I'm Detective Richard Marx with the LAPD. I'm working with Detective Ostrich on this case."

Grace shook his hand slowly, exchanging a glance with Nelson, who was chewing on his mustache determinedly.

"Nice to meet you," Grace said. "Last album not selling that well, or are you moonlighting just for fun?"

Nelson sputtered. Officer Marx stared at her blankly, and Grace winced. "Sorry. I make stupid jokes when I'm under stress. And it's just, you know…Richard Marx…"

Detective Marx's brow furrowed in obvious confusion, and Nelson and Grace blinked at one another in amazement. "Richard Marx is a musician," Nelson said. "Had some hits in the eighties. *Wherever you go, whatever you do—*"

"Oh, yeah, I think I've heard that one." The cop shook Nelson's hand.

"You never knew you shared a name with a famous singer?" Nelson asked.

"Never heard of him, to tell you the truth." Detective Marx slid into the bench seat across from them. He kneaded his thighs as his chubby, boyish face fell into grave lines. "So, your friend has been kidnapped?"

Grace nodded, then tremblingly launched into the story once more as the cop took notes on his cell phone.

Grace felt eyes watching her from the darkness outside the restaurant's windows, and slid further into the booth, trying to stay out of sight.

As she finished her narrative, the waiter came to take the detective's order. He got a pork torta mojada, coffee, and a caramel flan. Grace was glad he'd be all fueled up for the stakeout, at least.

The cop crunched a mouthful of chips. "So, fill me in here," he said. "Why does the kidnapper want your laptop?"

Grace explained about the article she wrote about Inez, and the follow-up interview she'd recorded in the hospital. "They must have somehow known about it, even though it had just happened."

The detective stared at her, a fragment of chip stuck to his bottom lip. "That was *you* who wrote that article about Inez Carter?"

Grace felt her eye twitch. "Wait, you didn't know that this case was related? Detective Ostrich didn't tell you?"

The cop sputtered like a clogged sprinkler. "I just got pulled onto this case, and barely know anything." He laughed. "This is awesome. I'm such a huge Karma Korn fan."

Grace scowled at her hands. "So," she said weakly, "you heard about the article on Fox News or something?"

He made a derisive noise as he typed something into his cell phone. "Fox News is so phony. I saw the story on Buzzfeed." He looked up from his cell, his eyes narrowing as he gazed at Nelson. "Hey, wait, aren't you like the bass player or something?"

Nelson twiddled his thumbs. "Drummer."

The detective let out a high-pitched cackle. The old man watching soccer craned his neck to look at him, flinched, then turned back to the TV, leaving off his commentary and hunching down in his chair.

"Holy shit, excuse my French," the cop said. His thighs made a meaty noise as he slapped them. "I'm gonna kick Ostrich's ass for not telling me. He said I'd find something I liked about this case, but I figured it was just the witness was hot or something." He gestured at Grace. "I mean, no offense."

"No offense taken," Grace said with some uncertainty. Nelson regarded the cop as if he were something that had just scuttled out from under the fridge.

Marx laughed again. "Woo. When the media get a hold of this one, I'm going to be giving interviews left and right."

Nelson and Grace gazed at each other in desperation. "But, right now," Grace said slowly, "you're not going to say anything to the media and risk pissing off the kidnappers. You're going to just try to solve the case, right?"

The cop heaved around in his seat. "Of course, of course. So. Anyway." He cleared his throat. "The kidnapper must have known about this Inez Carter interview, even though it wasn't published yet?"

"I haven't even written it yet," Grace said. "I'd just finished recording it about forty-five minutes before I got the call."

Detective Marx scratched his chin. The waiter trotted out with the coffee and a steaming plate piled high with pork torta. He danced carefully around Marx as if Marx were a hair-trigger landmine as he set the plates down, then he escaped back to the kitchen.

The detective missed the waiter's nervousness: he only had eyes for the food. He picked up his knife and fork and poked a huge bite of sandwich into his mouth, looking thoughtful as he chewed. "Who knew about this interview, then?" he said amidst an explosion of crumbs. "Who had the inside information?"

"Nelson and I," Grace said. "Inez of course, and Nicole Watters. Lyssa Medlin was in the hospital room, but that was after I was done with the interview, and I don't think we mentioned it. That's all I know of."

"Inez or Nicole must have told someone about it," Nelson quickly added, "or else someone has spyware on Grace's phone."

Marx chewed his cud. "It's possible. I'd like to speak with Inez Carter, and Nicole Watters. Right away, if possible. If they told someone else about the interview, we need to know that immediately. We can have your cellphone analyzed, but it's much more likely it's a word-of-mouth thing."

Grace and Nelson looked at each other, then quickly away again; the cop would probably have come up with an excuse to talk to Inez and Nicole even if they had zero connection to the case. But he did have a point. Nelson picked up his phone reluctantly. "I'll text them right now."

Marx took another bite of torta and wiped the sweat from his brow with a paper napkin. "So, um…you know… I heard that Inez almost got arrested by the Department of Homeland Security because she went through the airport scanners with 'Fuck you TSA' spelled out in metal sequins on her belly. Is that true?"

Grace sighed.

"I wouldn't say she was almost arrested," Nelson said, keeping his eyes on his phone. It dinged. "Inez and Nicole are on their way."

Detective Marx's phone dinged in turn, and he extracted it from the pocket of his professionally faded jeans. A grin spread across his face. "Ho, ho," he guffawed. "Ho, ho."

Nelson raised his eyebrows.

"What happened?" Grace asked.

The detective turned his phone around so they all could see. It was a video clip. He pushed play, and Grace and Nelson leaned forward over the cluttered table to watch.

The heavily-made-up face of a smiling brunette anchorwoman appeared. "More news from the front lines of the Karma Korn fiasco this evening. We've just received breaking news that rising star and accomplished musician

Zeus Mahoney, alleged love interest of Inez Carter, has been poisoned."

Grace put her hands over her face and peeked out between her fingers. A picture of Zeus hanging from the chandelier playing guitar floated across the screen, then another of him holding a cup of electric Kool-Aid and winking theatrically at the camera. They'd probably been taken by one of the zonked-out kids at the rave, and Grace wondered how they'd gotten a hold of it.

"Mahoney and Carter's alleged relationship has ignited a firestorm of internet controversy," the reporter continued during the overlay of photos. "Carter is a celebrated figurehead of the LGBTQ community, and is self-described as a lesbian, so some have speculated that the rumor is a lie spawned by anti-LGBTQ sentiment. Others suggest that Ms. Carter has been lying about her sexuality. The LAPD reports that the poisoning may be related to this controversy."

A familiar face appeared on the screen: *Detective James L. Ostrich, LAPD* was laid out in a banner below his smug expression. "It appears that Mister Mahoney ingested some chocolates heavily laced with narcotics, which were delivered to his residence," Detective Ostrich said. "We are following a few leads at the moment and hope to have the culprit in custody soon."

Grace scowled. "The chocolates were for me."

Nelson rolled his eyes. "But they wouldn't be able to talk about Inez's sordid love life if they said that."

Marx's eyes lit up feverishly. "Sordid?"

They ignored him. The scene cut back to the anchorwoman. "Anyone with information about this crime is urged to call the police hotline-"

Detective Marx jabbed a button, cutting off the video. "Ho, ho," he laughed again, shaking his head. "Ostrich is going to lord this over us until after Christmas."

"You can't talk to the media about the kidnapping," Grace blurted, gripping the edge of the table. "They told me not to go to the cops. You can't leak this story."

The detective's face grew serious. "Now, calm down, we're not talking to the media about this. The poisoning was separate."

Grace rubbed her temples, willing herself to not lunge over the table and grab the cop by what passed for his neck. The detective started flipping through his phone again, smiling faintly. Nelson flagged down the waiter and ordered another beer. When it came, he handed it to Grace with a significant look.

She took a large swig. "Thanks."

Nelson turned to the cop, crossing his arms. "What leads do you have in the poisoning case? You went through my credit card records to verify it wasn't me who sent the chocolates, right? Have you got any other leads, like it says on the video?"

"And have you talked to that Gary guy yet?" Grace asked.

The detective's brow furrowed as he shoved in another mouthful of food, clicking through his phone with his other hand. "Ostrich sent me the report, let me read it."

Grace chugged her beer as he read, mentally composing a scathing article about the LAPD. She'd write and publish it after Zeus was back safe and sound. Could you leave nasty reviews of police departments on Yelp?

The cop took another bite before speaking again, apparently unable to express himself unless it was through a mouthful of food. "We didn't find any evidence that you purchased the chocolates, Nelson. We spoke to the people at the shop where the flowers and candy came from and accessed their phone records. It looks like the person who ordered them called from one of those burner phones. The flowers were delivered to a hotel room downtown, and whoever it was must have laced the chocolates and then had them delivered by courier. We're trying to access video surveillance records at the hotel the flowers and candy were originally delivered to, and at your motel, to find out who the courier was so we can question them."

Grace and Nelson cursed. "So we're no closer to knowing who it was?" he asked.

"We're working on it," the detective said. "Warrants take time."

"What about Gary?" Grace asked.

"One of our detectives made contact with him. He's definitely a person of interest, but there's no hard evidence connecting him to any of this."

"He's a person of interest, all right," Grace said under her breath, taking another swig of beer.

The bell's jingle signaled the door opening again, and Nicole and Inez came in. The old man at the television finally turned away from the match to watch the progress of their swaying hips, looking as if Jesus had appeared carrying a keg of beer and a basket of pork rinds.

Inez wiped her red eyes, her pouty lips trembling. "Oh, my God, I can't believe someone kidnapped him." She let out a wet, snorting sob.

Nicole put a resigned arm around her. "Have you heard anything else since you texted us?"

Grace shook her head. Nicole frowned.

Inez gave Detective Marx a long, faintly disgusted look before sliding into the booth next to him. The proprietor hurried up with an extra chair for Nicole. His expression was manically polite as he took Inez and Nicole's orders—Cokes, and a burrito for Inez—then came back with more chips and salsa.

Detective Marx's face glowed as he gazed at the two young women. "So, uh," he said. "Uh."

Inez gazed at him and sniffed with a sound like someone taking a bong hit. "Uh?"

Nelson kneaded the back of his neck with his fingertips.

"Inez, Nicole, this is Detective Richard Marx."

Inez stopped sniffing. She and Nicole blinked. "Richard Marx?" Inez said. "Are you frigging serious?"

"We've been though that," Nelson said. "Moving on."

"So, anyway, I wanted to ask you a few questions," the cop said, wiping his forehead again with his now-sopping napkin. "First of all, the interview Inez gave Grace today—who did you talk about that with? Who else knew about it, besides the people in this room?"

"I didn't tell anyone," Inez said.

Nicole frowned deeper. "Me, either."

"Didn't post about it on social media, or anything like that?" Marx asked.

Nicole shook her head, rolling her eyes slightly. "That article will get enough publicity without my help."

"Duke banned me from personally posting on social media at all anymore," Inez said. "He says I project the wrong image when I'm being myself."

Grace's heart sank. Calling the cops had effectively just added more monkeys to the circus, and they were running out of bananas. If all Detective Marx was going to do was ogle Inez and compose the script for his next television interview, she'd have been better off with no backup at all. "So, what's the plan?" she asked. "I'm going to go dump my laptop at midnight, and then what?"

"We'll have undercover police stationed around the drop site," Marx said. "They'll stay and watch who picks up the items, and then we'll have them."

"Won't the kidnappers be expecting that?" Grace asked with rising panic.

Marx slurped his coffee. "You'd be surprised. In my experience, most criminals aren't rocket scientists. They told you not to contact the police, and they're going to rely on you being scared enough that you won't."

"What if they don't pick up the laptop, though?" Nelson asked. "What if they just leave it in the trash bin to be hauled off by the garbage truck?"

"The kidnappers said they'd call you with further instructions after the drop, correct?" Marx said. "We'll put a trace on your phone so we can catch them that way if they don't show themselves at the dumpster."

Inez examined a tendril of her turquoise hair with her red eyes and giggled nervously. "The Kidnappers would be a great name for a band." Nicole rolled her eyes and took Inez's hand. It struck Grace, even amidst all this bullcrap, that they were actually a pretty cute couple.

The waiter came back, placing a gigantic burrito in front of Inez and clearing away the now-spectacular piles of empty plates and flotsam. Inez puffed out her cheeks as he left. "Whoa, that's a hurkin' load of burrito. I'm gonna have to take extra diet powder after I eat this."

Nelson's face twisted slowly into a quizzical scowl. "Diet powder?"

Inez picked up her fork. "Yeah. It's this stuff you snort

that makes you not hungry. It's good and buzzy."

Nicole's jaw dropped. "You mean *cocaine?*"

"Pish," Inez said. "No. It's some stuff from the internet that you can only buy with Bitcoins because it's experimental." She gave the cop a nervous glance, but Richard Marx was immersed in looking at his cell phone and didn't see it. "It's totally legal, though. I mean, it's not really for human consumption, but it's legal. Tristan turned me onto it. I'm gonna have to figure out how to get it myself now that he quit working for Duke."

Nelson's face went crimson. "What the…I can't even… how long has this been going on?"

"Chill, Nels," Inez said as she dug into her food. "It's no big deal. I've been doing it since I signed on with Duke, and I'm fine. It's just to keep myself camera-ready. Apparently all this 'healthy weight' and 'positive self-image' crap is well and good for normal people, but no one wants to see a fatty rock star waggling around like a jiggly hippo. Look at all the crap bigger women get. I don't wanna deal with all that."

Nicole had the expression of someone who'd just sat in a pile of cat shit. Nelson looked in danger of bursting into flame. "Did Duke know about this?" Nelson asked. "Or was it just Tristan's idea?"

Inez shrugged and swallowed her huge mouthful of burrito. "Dunno. I never talked to him about it."

"I'm going to have a little chat with the Dukester," Nelson muttered.

"Me, too," Nicole said, crossing her arms. "Baby, your butt is cute, but it'd be cute if it was rounder, too."

"Awwww." Inez grinned, wiped the grease from her lips, and kissed her girlfriend. There was a clatter from over near the television; the guy watching soccer had dropped his can of beer. Officer Richard Marx reddened like a baked ham.

Something pricked at the back of Grace's mind. "Inez, I've been wondering—are you close with Tristan?"

Inez hacked at her burrito with her fork. "Not really. He was just Duke's guy, you know?"

"Why did he visit you in the hospital, then?" Grace asked.

Inez boofed. "Oh, that. Yeah, I guess he's opening his own talent agency. He wanted me to sign on with him instead, but I told him no. Too many lawyers and paperwork and whatever, and Dingus Duke doesn't do that bad of a job, after all. But Tristan came to ask again when I was in the hospital. Maybe he thought I'd be drugged up enough to say yes, but I wasn't, unfortunately."

A prickle spread over Grace's scalp. Tristan would have known where Inez was staying and would have had the means to overdose her on heroin disguised as "diet powder." "Inez, was it Tristan who came to your hotel that day you overdosed?"

Inez' face screwed up in concentration, then relaxed. "Still can't remember." She giggled. "You think that little emo bitch would try to kill me? I mean, yeah, he's kind of creepy, but why would he do that?"

"Maybe if he couldn't have you as a client, he didn't want Duke to either," Grace said uncertainly.

"But then why would he go after *you*, Grace?" Nelson asked.

"That I don't know." Grace tapped her fingertips on her beer bottle.

Officer Marx's phone binged with an incoming text. He read it, then looked up and put on his dignified cop face, the effect dampened somewhat by the burrito sauce on his cheek. "That's a message from Ostrich. It seems that we have a pretty good idea who the suspect is now."

They drew in a collective breath. "Who is it?" Grace asked.

"We were able to identify the IP address where the threatening Twitter messages came from right before Ms. Carter was poisoned." The dollop of sauce began to drip toward his chin. "It was that Gary character you told us about. The art gallery owner."

The momentary excitement squeezed out of Grace, replaced by incredulity. "Really? That's…actually a bit surprising."

Inez squinted at them. "Who's Gary?"

"You remember that guy who wanted photos with you, that first day we met you in the studio?" Grace asked.

Inez stared at her, her mouth slowly curling into an

incredulous smirk. "*That* guy? The little dweeb that smells like medicated foot powder?"

"That's the one."

"That's gnarly. How would that little goober kidnap Zeus? Zeus could bend him over his knee and spank him."

"He must have had help." Grace tried to picture Gary the Gnome pulling off a string of high-powered felonies because he was torqued about some article. She still couldn't; apparently she was an even worse judge of character than she thought, because that evidence sounded pretty damning. *This time the red herring was the one whodunit.* Her heart sank. Zeus, as usual, had been right. Now if only she could get him back so he could dance around and sing "Told you so."

She turned to Marx. "You're going after him right now, right? These crimes must be related. He must have Zeus." She was trembling again. Nicole patted her hand, and Nelson put his arm around her.

"Two officers were dispatched to his residence to take him into custody," Marx said. "We're waiting to hear back."

"How long will it take?" Grace asked.

"Not long. It's high-priority, and they'll get right on it."

So they waited. Officer Marx plowed through his flan. Inez declared defeat a third of the way through her burrito. Grace wiggled in her seat and fought the urge to get up and drive to Gary's herself. It was, if anything, more nerve-wracking to know who had Zeus and be unable to take any action. She was about to do jumping jacks to wear off some energy (she could only imagine the look on the waiter's face) when Richard Marx's phone blinged.

The cop puffed out his cheeks as he read it. "There was no one there."

They all groaned, and Grace felt like she was about to faint. "So, what are we going to do? What's going to happen?"

"We have an officer stationed at the location watching in case they come back, but it's likely the suspect has your friend Zeus at another location. We think at this point we should still plan on going forward with the laptop drop, to see if we can get them out of hiding or get other leads as to where they're holed up at. If we make contact with the suspect and find Zeus beforehand, then we'll call it off, of course."

Grace nodded, her heart pounding. She was trying to feel relieved that they'd at least identified the culprit, but she was just as worried as ever. "I'll do whatever you want me to do," she said.

Marx gave her a compassionate nod. "Thank you for your cooperation and patience. We're working hard on this, and I'm sure we'll have this Gary under wraps and your friend back safe and sound within a few hours. You have the best guys in the LAPD on the case, after all."

Inez stared at the cop, transfixed. "You have sauce on your cheek."

Marx went an overbaked shade, and he swiped at his face with the napkin.

"Other cheek," Inez said. "No, down. No, over." She huffed, grabbed the napkin from his hand and wiped the sauce away.

"Thank you." Marx looked back at Grace, still rosy as a valentine. "Anyway, the complete plan for tonight is in place. So here's what we're all going to do…"

Grace listened to the final details, wondering if this pork pie of a cop named after a mediocre musician could possibly save her friend.

***

After installing spyware on her phone to trace incoming calls (a procedure she hoped would be reversible, if this ordeal were ever over), Officer Marx insisted Grace return to her motel to wait for the midnight drop alone, in case her room was being watched.

So, she did. She tried to watch TV, but ended up pacing the floor, clutching her phone, waiting for Detective Marx to call and tell her they'd found Zeus. But the glowing red numbers clicked by on the alarm clock, inching toward midnight, and the call didn't come.

By the time eleven p.m. rolled around, she was practically banging against the walls like the agitator in a can of spray paint. She sighed and grabbed her purse. She'd be way early, but at least driving would give her something to do.

As she wove through the dark streets, she couldn't dispel the feeling she was missing something. She had no idea what Gary's motive was. Was he just lashing out at whoever struck his maniac fancy at the time? Was he trying to take out anyone he saw as damaging to the LGBTQ community? People had done crazier things, Grace reasoned.

If that were the case, it was possible he was just using Zeus to lure her in. Was Zeus already dead, and she his next intended victim? A shudder ran through her. If Zeus were dead, it might be easier to let Gary murder her, because she'd sure as hell never forgive herself.

She pushed back hard at the hollowness sucking the breath from her chest. Life without Zeus would be boring. Colorless. Too quiet. Tears came to her eyes as she remembered every time she'd told him to calm down and act normal, or had been annoyed by his antics.

"Stop it!" she said out loud. "He's not..." She swallowed. *He's fine. He'll be back before the night is over.*

Grace longed for simpler times when her biggest professional hazard was getting drenched by the Seattle rain on the walk from her car to a music venue.

By the time she pulled onto East Fourth Street, her palms were sweating and she fighting the dry heaves. Her dashboard clock said she had nearly fifteen minutes to kill before she was supposed to make the drop, and she didn't want to risk dumping the laptop early and messing up the plan somehow. So she cruised past the dark, barred windows of Sally's

Kitchen and up the block, past carnicerías and 99-cent stores, a few glum patrons visible through the grimy windows of all-night donut shops. She wondered idly if she should go buy Zeus a maple bar before realizing she may never have the chance to buy Zeus a maple bar again. It was all she could do to not succumb to a wave of unendurable anguish.

When her dash clock read five till, she turned around and headed back toward the drop site.

The back parking lot of Sally's Kitchen was a bare patch of littered gravel ringed by tortured chain link. It was completely deserted. There was a car lot on one side, a discount furniture store on the other, and a squat, stucco building that looked like cheap apartments to the rear. Grace scanned the shadows and windows, searching for hidden watchers, but didn't see anyone, not even the police that were supposed to be there. Her dashboard clock now read twelve-oh-one.

A chill ran up her spine: what if something had gone wrong, and the police weren't here? What if they'd made the dubious decision to concentrate all their manpower watching Gary's house? She tried to tell herself they weren't that stupid, but Detectives Ostrich and Marx didn't inspire confidence.

Grace squared her shoulders and took a deep breath. No point worrying about it now.

The Sally's Kitchen dumpster sat against the back wall of the restaurant, next to a steel-screened door. Grace parked alongside it and got out, leaving her engine running.

She felt unseen eyes on her back as she walked toward

the dumpster and resisted the urge to cower or run. She hoped she didn't faint in the dirty gravel like some dollar store version of a Victorian heroine.

The smell of trash assaulted her as she lifted the dumpster's lid. She hesitated a moment, hoping that Detective Marx would make good on his word to retrieve her computer after she'd dropped it. She'd backed up all the files to a thumb drive, just in case, but she didn't have anything like enough money to get a new laptop.

She closed her eyes and slipped the computer in, wincing at the wet squelching noise it made when it hit bottom; the best-case scenario was she'd be working on a laptop that smelled like rotten French fries for a while. Worst case, she and Zeus would be beyond the need for laptops, smelly or otherwise.

Grace scampered back to her car, her heart hammering. She kept thinking she saw movement in the shadows, but no one jumped out and grabbed her. She flung herself into the driver's seat, slammed the door shut, and hit the lock button.

She strapped herself in with shaking hands. Her unsteady foot on the accelerator sent gravel flying as she skidded out of the parking lot.

Back on the quiet street, she checked her phone. No one had called or texted yet. Her limbs had turned into gummy worms, and she concentrated on not swerving onto the sidewalks.

Her car crept slowly back up East Fourth. She glanced around the dark streets, carefully watching every pedestrian, but they just seemed to be the usual assortment of bums and late-night wanderers. One car approached in the opposite lane, but it passed and didn't turn around.

Still, no one called.

She had no idea what to do now. Should she risk calling Nelson or the cops? But what if she missed Gary's call? She shoved her stubbornly silent phone into the breast pocket of her shirt. Why hadn't Detective Marx told her what to do if this happened? She could go home and wait, hoping someone would call her, but she'd never wanted to go home less in her life: she'd tear the walls apart.

Lost in her worries, she didn't see the car pull out from the alleyway until it was right in front of her.

Grace slammed hard on the brakes. Her car skidded sideways, her tires squealing; her front bumper came to a halt inches from the little sedan. Grace panted, her hand pressed over her heart.

The sedan was now parked at an angle in the middle of the street. A tall, broad-shouldered man climbed out of the driver's door. She saw a flash of his brown, slicked-back hair in her headlights before he passed back into shadow, circling around toward her door. Grace was wondering why someone would bother stopping for a near-accident, when the man pulled something from his waistband and there were two explosive pops, her car jolting with each one. As her vehicle listed towards the driver's side, Grace moaned in terror: those had been gunshots. The man had blown her tires out.

The figure approached her door. The reflected headlights glinted off the barrel of the gun in his hands, a silencer affixed to the end. Grace frantically scanned the cabin of her car, looking for a weapon. All she saw were crumpled taco wrappers, a forlorn box of snack mix, and a half-empty cup of curdled latte.

The man pressed the barrel against the driver's-side window, directly in line with Grace's head, and she wondered if throwing rotten latte on him would be gross enough to get him to drop the gun. He'd probably just shoot her in annoyance.

"Go ahead and unlock the door," the man said in a pleasant, Casey Kasem voice. It was vaguely familiar, but it definitely wasn't Gary's. Grace's brow furrowed.

"Why don't you just hurry up and unlock that door," the man repeated. "I'm sort of in a rush here."

Grace, shaking and sweating, not seeing any alternative, pushed the unlock button. She whimpered slightly as the door swung open.

The gun barrel greeted her, inches from her forehead. Behind it, incredibly straight, white teeth glowed in the low light.

"Why don't you just park your car and come with me," Duke said.

16

Grace sat trembling in the passenger seat of Duke's car, her hands and feet shackled with handcuffs. "It was *you* who kidnapped Zeus?" Grace asked unsteadily. "But…that doesn't make sense! What about Gary?"

Duke laughed. "Gary didn't have anything to do with kidnapping your little boyfriend. I just hacked his computer to send those tweets and throw people off. I knew the twerp would be upset about your article, so it was convenient."

Grace winced, remembering that Duke was Gary's boyfriend's agent. How had she not seen that connection? "Do you have a trace on my phone? How did you know I gave that interview?"

Duke raised his eyebrows. "Inez told me."

"What?" Anger lodged in her throat. "Is she in on this?"

Duke waved his hand dismissively. "She's not smart enough to be in on this. I told her to keep a log of the times she talks to the media, and she's usually good about it. I keep an eye on that list, since it's backed up on the Cloud. It's a good thing, too. Otherwise her career would be toast." He shook his head and rolled his eyes. "Girl has no idea how to effectively market herself."

Grace's teeth clenched. If she ever got out of this, she'd smack Inez silly. "Is Zeus okay? You haven't hurt him, right?"

Duke slicked back his hair. The gun—a huge, shiny silver revolver that looked like something Clint Eastwood would carry—lay in his lap. "We haven't hurt him yet."

Grace twisted and tugged at the handcuffs behind her back. "Please let Zeus go. I'll do whatever you want."

Duke didn't answer. He was scowling at the GPS map in the dashboard. "That's the most idiotic route in the world. Who programs these things?"

The dash lights and passing streetlights blurred with Grace's desperate and furious tears. "Why are you doing this? I don't understand."

"You were causing so much trouble for my clients, and it's my job to protect their reputations. What was I supposed to do?"

"Protect their reputations? You drugged Inez. You did it with that 'diet powder' Tristan had been giving her, right?"

Duke grinned. "Guilty! It was a pretty good plan, especially since Inez didn't even remember me coming over. But I would have convinced her it was accidental and to keep her mouth shut even if she had remembered. She's such an airhead."

"How is killing her protecting her reputation?"

Duke sighed. "I never wanted her to *die*. Not yet, anyway. The return on that investment wouldn't have been prime. No, I was going to be the one who discovered her overdosed on her hotel room floor, but Nelson beat me to it." He shook his head with a smile. "That man guards her like she's a prize poodle, but really it's for all the wrong reasons."

"But why would you want her to overdose in the first place?"

Duke's wide, earnest eyes darted between the road and her face. "It was a spectacular opportunity. I fostered an excellent branding image—the persecuted lesbian, you know— and the publicity from it was stupendous. The sales of Karma Korn's new single are through the roof. Inez will definitely thank me for my creative marketing tactics someday. And, by the way, I want to thank you for publishing that slanderous article of yours, because it ended up being such a sales boon as well, once I'd given it the right spin." He gave her a little salute.

"If I'm such a frigging sales boon for you, why are you kidnapping us?"

Duke gave her a disappointed look, shaking his head. "You just wouldn't stop nosing around in my clients' business, causing more trouble. Eventually, it would get too hard to spin. I had to take further action."

Grace's forehead itched as sweat ran down in droplets. "Where do you have Zeus? What have you done to him?"

"You'll see him soon enough. Ooh, listen, it's Beatbot. She's so great, right?" He turned up the volume knob on the stereo.

Grace's phone buzzed with a text in her shirt pocket. She glanced over at Duke, who was trying to beat box along with the song. There was no way she could see who was texting her without him noticing, especially with the handcuffs on. Maybe he'd be stupid enough to leave her alone and she'd be able to call the police.

Had the cops and Nelson figured out something had happened to her yet? Had the police been trailing her after the computer drop? Grace checked the wing mirror and glanced quickly behind them, but she had no way of knowing if any of the headlights following them belonged to a cop car. If they knew she'd been kidnapped, why wouldn't they have tried to pull them over already? *Maybe they're waiting until Duke leads them back to where Zeus is.*

She cursed inwardly for not having the brains to ask beforehand if they'd be tailing her, or if they'd just be monitoring her phone. If they weren't watching her, it could be hours before anyone noticed she was gone.

"I love hearing my peeps on the radio," Duke said, pausing in his sputtering and raspberry-blowing to bop his head with the rhythm. "I love helping artists, creating their careers. It's such a wonderful feeling."

Grace leaned her head against the headrest and tried to keep herself from throwing up. "Why are you going through all this effort just to keep people from finding out Inez is pansexual? It's really not that big of a deal. People would like her music anyway."

He held up a hand. "Hold on, I'm listening." He cranked the volume knob even more.

When the song ended, Grace took her chance and spoke into the silence. "I dropped off my laptop, like you asked. I won't write any more articles. You have no reason —" The announcer's voice blasted through the speakers, drowning her out.

Duke sighed and turned down the volume. "But you called the police, after we asked you not to, so we had to switch it up a bit." He flicked her playfully on the arm, which was quickly cramping up from being handcuffed behind her back. "Wish you hadn't done that. It was really a bitch to rearrange our schedule."

Grace wondered who the other party or parties involved in the *we* were. Was that little creep Tristan working with him, even though he'd quit? Had quitting been a farce? "Did Inez log that we were meeting with the police, too?"

He frowned. "No, she didn't think to do that, which makes me a bit peeved. But we have a friend in the Department." He winked. The next track came on the radio: Karma Korn's "Nightmare Before Fish Sticks." Duke grinned wide, gesturing at the radio. "Would you listen to that? Speak of the devil." He laughed and turned up the volume again, singing along with Inez. Grace began to wish he'd just torture her physically.

After another ten minutes of hell, Duke took an onramp to the freeway, heading west toward Santa Monica.

"Where are we going?" Grace asked.

He drummed his manicured hands against the steering wheel. "A cute little rental of mine that happens to be vacant right now. I'd ask if you'd be interested in it, since you're living in that horrible motel room, but I really don't think you're a good credit risk at this point." He laughed.

They were in a part of the city Grace didn't know, and she watched the street signs, trying to memorize them. A few more minutes of being hammered by Duke's singing and they pulled up in front of a little adobe bungalow, a neglected palm hanging its head over the crispy lawn. Duke put the car in park and opened the driver's side door. "I'm going to come around and let you out. Don't try to scream or run for it. It won't even attract attention in this neighborhood, and besides: you won't get far." He waved merrily with the gun. Grace winced.

Duke ambled around the front bumper and opened her door. Grace swung her shackled legs out, stood up, and immediately toppled over.

Duke caught her with the hand not holding the gun, and her face mashed into his cologne-scented armpit. "Careful there," he said, hauling her upright. "Don't want to have to make an injury claim on my homeowner's." He guffawed. Grace wished her hands were free so she could punch him.

Duke held her elbow tightly as they headed for the front door, and she hobbled alongside him as best she could. The street was quiet. Lights shone through grubby sheets hung askew over several of the neighbors' windows, but it didn't seem likely someone would look out and see her. Besides, Duke was right: in this neighborhood, a man leading a shackled woman into his house probably wasn't a strange enough occurrence to warrant calling the law.

Duke unlocked the front door. It opened onto a living room furnished only with a lumpy, overstuffed sofa and cheap glass coffee table. The walls were bare, and the smell of dog wafted from the mangy brown carpet. A shrill squeaking emanated from somewhere in the back. "I'm home," Duke called cheerfully as he locked the door again behind him. "I got her."

Zeus's voice rang from the back of the house. "Gracie? Is it Gracie?"

Grace let out a sigh. "Zeus!"

"Gracie! These people are weird, you really shouldn't have come."

Tears sprang to Grace's eyes. Duke nudged her forward, through a tiled kitchen with a sink full of dishes, into a small, grim bedroom.

Zeus bounced on the edge of a double bed, the cheap metal frame creaking, which was the source of the noise Grace had heard. His hands were cuffed in front of him. Sitting next to him on the rumpled navy blue comforter, a

Glock on her freckled knees and an expression of extreme annoyance on her face, was Marla Pocchino.

Marla lazily cocked an auburn eyebrow, her body jiggling with the bed's motion. "Hey, Grace."

Grace's stood frozen, her eye twitching. "It *was* you." She spat a curse. "That's how you keep getting your stupid stories. *Duke* has been feeding you information."

Marla's large, soft, unpainted lips curled in answer. Zeus bounced higher, the bedframe squealing in protest, and Marla steadied the gun on her knees so it didn't bounce off. "Having good contacts is the cornerstone of successful journalism," she said.

"You're not a successful journalist, you're a fucking fraud."

Marla just rolled her eyes, her shoulders rising and falling like an equestrian's as she rode the bouncing bed.

"These ugly dorks came to the hospital to get me," Zeus said a little breathlessly, his butt actually getting airborne now with each bounce. "It was gnarly. They pulled their guns and told me to keep quiet, just like in one of those action movies about diamond heists or government agents foiling terrorist plots. Except I'm not a diamond or a terrorist."

Marla rubbed her temples, shooting Duke a poisonous look, and Grace gleefully imagined her as Zeus's sole audience for many long hours. "I'm so glad you're okay, Zuzu," Grace said.

He kept bouncing, his eyes locked on hers. "This is a fun game, but I want to play with someone else now."

Grace mouth tightened, and she turned to Duke. "I still don't get why we're here."

Duke shoved the revolver into the waistband of his expensive jeans like a television street thug, except on him it looked goofy. Grace hoped he'd shoot his dick off. "Well, see, I've built Inez Carter's career by casting her as a valiant champion of gay rights," Duke explained. "It's a very popular narrative in today's social climate. These Millennials and Gen Z kids are willing to spend gobs of money downloading that story's soundtrack." He puffed out his tanned cheeks. "But then *you* come in and insert this unpopular subplot. The gay-activist narrative gets pretty watered down if the heroine's sexuality is called into question. So, I tried to get the plot back on track, making it look like you were some homophobic hater telling lies. It would have worked fantastically; the bullied-homosexual-committing-suicide storyline is really big right now, and the outpouring of support from the community was amazing. But you wouldn't give up, so I had to fix things."

"So you tried to poison me, and got Zeus instead," Grace said.

Duke shrugged. "A narcotics overdose in a seedy L.A. motel, which you were living in with your…emotionally disturbed young foster son, would have satisfied the public appetite for the grotesque. It would have completely discredited you posthumously and gotten Inez and Nicole even more press and sales. But, as you know, that plan didn't work either." He sighed. "So, on to another plan. What are we going to do with you now?"

"We should go get some pizza," Zeus said. "That sounds like the best plan to me. I know a place with a great arcade over by our motel. It has this really killer ninja game, and I always kick Gracie's ass at it. I'll bet I could beat both of you, too."

Marla finally snapped, her languorous demeanor evaporating in an instant. "Will you please *shut up* and *quit bouncing?*"

"No," Zeus said.

Marla gestured violently. "Can't we just kill them *now?*"

Duke tsked. "That wouldn't play as well. Just be patient."

She tossed her professionally styled hair. "Why did we have to kidnap the whole short bus? This is so annoying."

Zeus's brow furrowed, and he slowly bounced to a stop, his head hanging. He hated it when people insinuated he was stupid, the r-word. It was something his mom had always said. Grace vowed to herself that, if she ever got out of this, she'd eat garlic chili every day and cut a deal with the Department of Corrections to let her into Marla's cell for an epic fart-and-depart.

"What *is* our plan, anyway?" Marla asked Duke. "I'd like to get this over with so I can get home. I just want to curl up with a bowl of quinoa casserole and binge-watch *Justified* right now."

"That sounds heavenly," Duke said. "I've got to take Millie to the groomers, but I can come over after and join you. I'll bring that olive fig dip I make."

Marla looked like he'd offered to grind her nose off with a belt sander. "Sure, that'd be awesome."

Duke turned his sparkling grin on Grace. "As for what we're going to do with you…what we *were* going to do was shackle you to the bed. You know, film a little sex video of you with your little foster son here. It would have made a great article, about how you were trying to blackmail Inez Carter with false claims about her sexuality while working in league with your little weirdo boyfriend. Everyone loves a good sex video, especially when it's a woman with her retarded foster son. But, unfortunately, you went to the police, so we'll have to change plans."

"Zeus isn't retarded," Grace spat, her hands curling to fists behind her back.

"I have a whole pile of brains," Zeus said with an evil little grin and what Grace thought of as his deliberately-crazy stare. "Some of them are even mine."

That stare didn't unnerve them like it did some people. "However many piles of brains you have," Marla said, "I'm going to shoot them all to pieces if you don't shut the hell up."

Duke held his palms up. "Now calm down, Marla. We can't shoot anyone's brains. That would just play into the story the cops have bought into, that this is a kidnapping-blackmail-type situation. I'm actually thinking heroin overdose for both of them is the way to go."

Marla nodded. "It's a little overdone in this narrative, but it *is* the L.A. way to die."

"Precisely. And I can leave the prepaid phone we used to make the blackmail call and all the other evidence with the bodies, so it's clear they concocted the whole kidnapping scam themselves. It'll be a *great* story. We can really milk the publicity."

Marla picked a speck of something off her gun. "That sounds like a pretty solid plan."

Zeus's eyes went wide, and he fidgeted with the chain of his handcuffs. "You people are crazy. This situation you're creating is bigtime, mega balls all around."

"The police are still going to trace this back to you," Grace said, trying to keep her voice from shaking. "They're going to wonder where I went, and they'll come looking. You'll get off easier if you let us go."

Duke waved a dismissive hand. "They won't come looking. I paid off some guys to lay a false trail. One of them is going to fish your laptop out of that dumpster, the other one texted your phone, pretending to be the kidnapper. They're going to give the police information that will make it look like they were hired by you, too."

Grace swallowed hard, trying not to let her last hope drain out. Duke was smarter than he looked. "The police will still figure it out. You really think you can trick the LAPD?"

Marla snorted and Duke burst out laughing.

Grace winced; they had a point. "You don't have to kill us, I swear," Grace begged. "We'll tell the police Zeus was just pulling a prank with the kidnapping stuff. I won't print more articles. I'll leave the city and get a job at McDonalds. Whatever you want. Just let us go."

"I'm afraid that would bring hardly any publicity at all," Duke said. "Heroin overdose is the best thing for my clients and for everyone involved. Except maybe you, of course."

"If you're going to kill us anyway, can we at least do the thing where we chain Gracie to the bed and I have sex with her first?" Zeus asked.

Grace grimaced. "Zeus, for fuck's sake…"

"Chained naked to the bed *and* dead of a heroin overdose would make an even better story," Marla said. "But I'm not suffering through watching the sex part."

Duke stroked his chin, looking thoughtful. "I don't know, it could be interesting. And a sex tape would get *billions* of hits after they're dead."

Marla stomped her foot. "Duke!"

He held his hands up in surrender. "All right, all right, if you really don't want to…" He raised his eyebrows at her;

she huffed and crossed her arms. Duke shrugged. "Then I guess the only question is, where do we do this thing?"

Marla and Duke fell into a thoughtful silence. Grace sat down next to Zeus, putting her head on his shoulder. They were both trembling. "What are we going to do, Gracie?" Zeus whispered.

"We'll think of something. Don't worry, Zuzu." She raised her head and smiled at him, and he smiled back. The look of trust and confidence in his eyes made her want to sink into the earth, because she had zero ideas how to get out of this situation.

Marla snapped her fingers. "Let's get them a room at the Ritz-Carlton. I know a guy who works there. He can make arrangements so they can't trace the charges or anything back to us." She broke into a wide grin, her green eyes sparkling with enthusiasm. "Ooh, ooh! I have a better idea. I'll call my friend, you know, the guy who works for Miley Cyrus? We can make it so the hotel room expense is traced back to her account. It'll look like she was helping them, out of jealousy about Inez's career, you know? Kill three nerds with one stone."

Duke clapped his hands and laughed heartily, his perfect teeth glinting. "I love it! And afterwards we can stop for a bite at that little all-night bistro that's right there. You know the one I mean, with the really good fondue?"

"Sure, we went there with Jesse and that guy he was dating, with the mole on his forehead."

Duke made a face. "Gross. I hope Jesse talked him into getting it removed. But how are we going to get them into the room without being seen? The police will ask the clerks questions and look at security cameras."

Marla shrugged. "We'll just talk to our friend Detective Phillip, right? He'll keep the investigation in hand."

Duke ruffled her strawberry locks. "Good thinking."

Marla pulled her cell from the pocket of her little anchor-buttoned shorts, and Duke pulled out his gun, scratching his chin with it before pointing it at Zeus and Grace.

Marla spoke into her phone. "Hey, Mister Mister. What's up?" She got up and wandered out of the room, her voice fading down the hall until it was an unintelligible mutter.

Duke gestured with the gun. "Let's go, peeps. Time to get up and get down."

Zeus exchanged a darting look with Grace, then they both slowly got to their feet. Tears came to Grace's eyes, because of how young and helpless Zeus looked. He'd had such a hard life, and it was about to end far too soon unless she suddenly came up with a plan. But nothing was coming to mind. As she followed Zeus out of the room and through the kitchen, Duke at their backs with the gun, she prayed desperately that the cops somehow had their shit together and were on their way.

They went out the door into the night. The street remained quiet: no witnesses peered out their windows, and no phalanx of squad cars blocked their retreat. Grace fought back dizziness as she traipsed down the cracked walk to the waiting car. If the cops had known where they were, they'd surely have arrived already. There was no reason for them to wait any longer. Grace imagined Detective Richard Marx still sitting in his unmarked car back by the dumpster, eating chips and listening to talk radio, and hot fury overtook her. How could they have assigned the biggest idiot in the LAPD to this case?

Duke shut them into the back of the car. In the moment they had alone, Zeus turned to Grace. "I love you, Gracie," he whispered.

She smiled sadly, tears running down her cheeks. "I love you too. We're going to be okay. We'll get out of this."

Zeus's eyes grew wide and lost as they stared into hers, and Grace tried hard to inject more confidence into her expression. He nodded, determination hardening his jaw.

Duke opened the driver's door, sighing as he settled into his seat. He pulled down the visor and checked his reflection in the mirror, smoothing his hair back. Marla came out of the house and trotted down the walk. She grinned as she strapped herself into the passenger seat. "Leroy is such a dork."

Duke started the engine. "Did you get it all worked out?"

"Sure did."

"Good girl. I can't wait to see the news feed on this. Miley Cyrus is going to be so pissed." They both giggled.

They got back on the highway, heading for downtown. Marla and Duke talked about some romantic comedy they wanted to see and discussed a trip to Sonoma. In the back, Zeus scooted over and leaned his head on Grace's shoulder. She rested her cheek on top of his head, closing her eyes. Every possible scenario of getting them out of this situation ran through her head, but most of them involved her possessing heretofore unknown kung fu skills.

The car dipped off the highway into a forest of skyscrapers. Marla pulled out her phone and punched out a text. "Drive around back," she said. "Leroy is waiting at the utility door."

They pulled around through the truck entrance to the back of the building. A baby-faced young man in an employee's uniform stood beside a small door next to a loading dock, rocking on his heels and smoking a cigarette. Marla jumped out of the car before Duke had even come to a complete stop and ran up to embrace her friend. They stood talking animatedly, Leroy grinning like an idiot and eyeing Marla's cleavage.

Duke got out and came around to open Grace's door. "Now, I'm going to take off your handcuffs and shackles, but don't bother trying anything funny. I've still got my trusty buddy Mr. Gun here." He patted the bulge under the hem of his shirt.

"I'm not a friend of Mr. Gun," Zeus said sadly.

Duke unlocked Grace's wrists and ankles, then leaned over to get Zeus's wrists. Grace stretched her arms, working the blood back in, her eyes on the gun in Duke's waistband. She pictured her hand darting out snakelike to grab it, tossing it aside and crying "Hiya-owwwwwaawaa!" as she karate-chopped him in the throat. Duke would collapse on the floorboards of the car, spurting a geyser of gore, and Grace would grin maniacally at him as he died.

Duke put a hand on the butt of his gun, tsking. "Now just don't, Grace. You know better." He finished unlocking Zeus and stood beside the open car door, glancing around at the dumpsters and loading bays with an expression of affected seriousness, his hand still resting pompously on the butt of Mr. Gun. "Get on out now, you two. Nice and slow."

They climbed out, Grace stretching her cramped limbs. The smell of exhaust and trash permeated the muggy air. Marla's throaty giggle rose above the noise of the hotel's HVAC pump as she fake-flirted with Leroy.

Duke marched them up a short flight of concrete steps, bringing up the rear. Marla and her friend fell silent and watched them approach, the man examining Grace and Zeus with mild curiosity. He pulled a key out and unlocked the door, holding it open for them. "Welcome to the Ritz," he said with a smile.

Marla giggled. "You're such an ass, Leroy."

They passed into a storeroom stacked with boxes and piles of linens. Leroy handed Marla a key card, raising his downy eyebrows. "Twenty-fourth floor," he said. "Room one twelve."

Marla embraced him again, making a little fakey "mmmm" noise. "Thanks, Leroy."

Leroy swiped a keycard on a terminal next to the utility elevator, and the doors opened. Duke, Marla, Grace, and Zeus climbed into the dingy, scuffed interior, which smelled of cleaning products. Duke pressed the button for the twenty-fourth floor and Marla waved at Leroy as the doors closed.

"He seems like a nice guy," Duke remarked, peering at a chip in his buffed nails. "Where do you know him from?"

"We were in a writers' group together."

"Ah," Duke said, splaying his fingers and examining them further. "You two had a little thing going on?"

Marla scowled. "What does it matter? That was a long time ago."

"Just asking. I mean, you know, he looked quite a bit younger than you…"

"Not *quite a bit*, Duke." He opened his mouth again, and she glared, crossing her arms. "Let it go. It's none of your business."

He sighed. "All right, all right."

The elevator doors slid open again. Duke herded Zeus and Gracie out into another utility closet, then into the plush-carpeted hallway. "Again, don't think of making a fuss," he said softly. "You'll just get us booted out, and we'll have to murder you somewhere with a lower star rating. Here, at least the cockroaches won't eat you when you're dead."

Grace watched Marla's pert butt wiggle down the corridor. She figured screaming would definitely get someone's attention at this point, and if they were going to die anyway…

She opened her mouth, but before her lungs could fill, Duke's hand clamped around her mouth.

But Zeus had apparently had the same idea, and Marla wasn't as quick. "Help! We're being murdered!" Zeus yelled.

Grace was pulled backward as Duke lunged for Zeus. "FBI!" Zeus yelled, jumping away from Marla and trying to grab Grace's arm and pull her away from Duke. "ATF! CIA! AC/DC!" Marla tackled him, colliding with the other two. A confusion of bumps and tangled limbs ensued, and Gracie landed straight on her back, her air knocked out. There was a scuffling and muffled cries as Duke pulled Zeus into a headlock.

Marla dug a heel of her boaters into Grace's throat, the barrel of her pistol aimed at Grace's forehead. "Get up," she hissed. She glanced nervously around the empty hallway and shot Duke a venomous look. He sat on the floor, his muscles twitching with the effort of holding

Zeus's face against the carpet. Zeus's muffled protests still filled the hallway

"You can't keep them quiet for a few seconds?" Marla spat.

He glared at her as Zeus reached up to pull his hair. "It was *your* guy that screamed."

Marla huffed. She grabbed Grace by the arm and jerked her upright, then dragged her roughly the few remaining paces to room one twelve. Grace listened desperately for the sound of hotel doors opening, of footsteps running down the hall to save them, but all remained quiet. The guests were apparently unwilling to disturb their Ambien-induced slumber to get involved in some low-class kerfuffle in the hallway.

Marla swiped the key card furiously and pushed Grace inside the hotel room, sending her sprawling. Duke dragged a flailing Zeus in behind them and shut the door. "Ouch!" Duke yelped, pulling his hand from Zeus's mouth. "

"Help! We've been kidnapped by lunatics!" Zeus bellowed.

Marla stomped over and smacked Zeus across the head with her gun. Grace yelped, but her planned scream petered out as Marla put her gun against Zeus's temple.

The little bastard bit me!" Duke complained.

"What, you don't have your rabies shot?" Marla asked. "Quit complaining." She gave Duke a tight-lipped glare. "Gag Grace, I'll take care of this Gomer."

"What do you want me to gag her with?"

"Your goddamn johnson, I don't care." She whipped a washcloth off of the rack and jammed it in Zeus's mouth. "Keep quiet, or I'll blast your empty head apart."

Duke stuffed a washcloth into Grace's mouth, as well. The plush cloth pressed against her tongue, grating against her taste buds with the sour flavor of hotel laundry soap. Her heart thundered in her chest. No one had busted through the door to save them yet, so it seemed unlikely to happen. It was up to her to save them, and this thought brought panic bubbling into her throat. *Add being a hero to the list of things I'm no good at.*

Duke took Grace's wrists and pulled her through the sitting area and toward the king bed. "Marla, there's no bedposts. What am I supposed to handcuff her to?"

"Again, your dick would be fine," Marla said, pulling a stumbling Zeus with her. "Just fucking handcuff her for now, Duke. For God's sake. We can worry about putting the bodies in compromising positions after they're dead." Marla elbowed Zeus in the face, making him grunt and protest through the washcloth, before wrestling his arms behind his back. The motion pushed her gun out of her waistband and onto the floor, but Marla didn't seem to notice, her attention on her flailing captive. Duke was busy with Grace's handcuffs and didn't see, either.

Zeus did, though. He met Grace's gaze before he surreptitiously kicked the weapon and sent it skidding across the earthy brown carpet toward the closet door.

Marla sat on Zeus as she handcuffed his wrists, then his ankles, wrapping the cuffs' chains so he was bent in hogtie position with his belly on the floor. The washcloth in his mouth wiggled as he chewed on it, and his golden eyes met Gracie's again.

Gracie glanced toward the gun, but it was far out of their reach.

Duke handcuffed Grace's wrists behind her back, and her ankles, but didn't hogtie her. He leaned her against the bedside bureau like a sack of dog food. "Now what?"

Marla sniffed. She fished in her pockets and brought out a tiny baggie, a spoon, a lighter, and a syringe. She flung the stuff at Duke. "Here. Cook up their shots." Then she saw her gun laying on the ground and gave a little start of surprise. "Shit!"

Grace wilted. There went her last, faint hope. Marla picked her gun up and held it idly, placing her foot on Zeus's back. Zeus, his face red with the effort of holding his chin up, stared at Grace intensely, still chewing on the washcloth. He looked like he was trying to communicate something to her, but she had no idea what it could possibly be.

Duke, muttering under his breath, picked up the drug paraphernalia. He took the spoon to the sink, opening the tap and splattering himself as the water ricocheted off the spoon. "Damn!" He turned the water down, then up, then down again, jostling the faucet handle as he tried to get the perfect dribble.

"Put some water in a fucking glass, and draw it up with the syringe, you moron!" Marla said. She gestured with the gun. "There's glasses right there, by the sink."

"Oh yeah." Duke filled a glass, took it over to the bed, and sat down. He rolled a little nugget of black tar into a spoon, drew water into the syringe and squirted it on the dope, his brow furrowed in concentration. He looked like a golden retriever trying to figure out a calculus problem.

Marla sighed and slammed the gun down on the bathroom counter, stomping over. "Give me that already." She wrested the spoon from his fingers. "Were you raised in a goddamn bible camp or something?"

"All right, all right," Duke said. "You don't have to get all snooty about it."

She sniffed, flicking the lighter under the spoon, the flame reflecting in her green eyes. The room filled with the pungent odor of cooking heroin, making Grace's eyes water. Marla mashed the dope up efficiently with the butt of the syringe, then tossed in a nugget of cotton and drew up a liquid the color of strong, black coffee. She grinned as she held the needle up, flicking the bubbles out with her French-tipped nails. "That ought to do them," she said. "Hold little Miss Grace's arm."

Duke sat beside Grace, still looking affronted, and grabbed her left wrist, twisting her forearm out. Marla knelt and prodded at the vein in the crook of Grace's arm with her fingertip. "There it is," she muttered. She poised the needle, and Grace closed her eyes tightly, squeezing out tears. *Maybe I'll survive it*, she thought. *Or maybe Zeus will survive, at least. Please God, or whoever...*

The needle pricked.

With her eyes closed, Grace didn't see what happened next. There was a thump and a crash and Marla screamed and fell onto Grace's chest, knocking her against the bureau.

Grace's eyes flew open wide, but all she could see was Marla's hair and flailing limbs. There was another crash, and Duke yelled. Marla's elbow caught Grace in the chin as she rolled off of her.

The door opened. A flurry of footsteps sounded on the soft carpet. "Freeze! Stop right there!"

Grace lay very still, looking up into the faces of a half-dozen police officers as they flooded into the room. Marla was sprawled, moaning, on the floor, her face bleeding freely, surrounded by shards of broken lamp. Duke crouched beside her, frozen with shock, gazing with wide eyes at the gang of cops.

Zeus lay in front of Grace, still hogtied. He spit out the washcloth and grinned. "Did you see my moves, Gracie? That was badass. Boosh! I got her!"

"How the hell did you—?"

But her question was cut off as police swarmed around

them, grabbing Duke and Marla and putting them in handcuffs. There was a confusion of voices and action, the room teeming with cops and EMTs, hotel staff and reporters in the hallway. Cameras flashed. A red-haired female officer unlocked Grace and Zeus's handcuffs.

Grace took Zeus in her arms, taking the first deep breath it seemed she'd had in ages.

"You two okay?" the red-haired officer asked, putting her hand on Zeus's shoulder. "We've got paramedics on the way."

"I'm fine," Grace said, holding Zeus tightly. "Zeus needs to be looked at though." She traced a bruise blooming on his swollen cheek.

"I'm okay, Gracie. I'm fine now."

"But that bitch hit you." Her eyes traveled to Marla, who was up against the hotel wall with an officer patting her down. *That treatment is too good for her*, Grace thought. *She deserves some police brutality.*

Zeus wove a strand of Grace's hair between his fingers. "I'm fine, Gracie. We're both okay now. It turned out all right, just like you said."

"Yeah," she gave a watery laugh. "Yeah, it did, thanks to you. If you hadn't kicked her or whatever, right when you did…"

Zeus frowned. "You didn't see?"

She winced. "No, Zeus. I had my eyes closed."

The frown disappeared. "That's cool. I can't watch when

they give me shots, either." He giggled. "It was too bad you missed it though. That was like the best moves of my life. I tumbled like a tumbleweed." He stopped laughing, his eyes going round and lost. "I thought she was going to kill you. I thought I was going to watch you die."

She took him in her arms again. Detective Ostrich waded through the crowd in the doorway and made a beeline for them. "Hello, Miss Morgan, Mister Mahoney. How are you feeling?"

Grace squinted at him, still clinging to Zeus. "Okay, I guess, under the circumstances."

The detective winced. "I'm sorry it took us so long to get here. We were questioning other suspects…that guy Gary for one. It wasn't adding up. He denied sending the threatening messages, and he'd been at an opening at one of his galleries at the time Zeus was kidnapped."

"Yeah, Duke told me he hacked Gary's computer and sent those messages himself."

Detective Ostrich nodded. "Then we noticed that the GPS tracking signal on your phone had you somewhere you shouldn't be. When we found your car with the tires shot out, we put two and two together."

Grace let out a breath. "You were tracking my phone. Thank God."

The detective nodded. "Yes, but just with the 'find friends' feature, not with any tracking device. It was your friend Nelson who brought it to our attention that you had gone AWOL."

"Nelson did that?" Grace asked.

Ostrich smiled. "He insisted pretty firmly that we go after you immediately, that you didn't just go driving off on your own, and it's good he did. Looks like we got here just in time."

Grace leaned her forehead on Zeus's shoulder. "It would have been too late, if it weren't for Zeus." She looked at him. "You saved my life."

Zeus blinked at her. "You've saved mine a million times."

17

Nelson's biceps bulged as he hauled Grace's heavy tube amp out of the storage unit. He set it gently at her feet, smiling. "Got it all?"

"Yeah, that should be it."

He put his arm around her waist, kissing her temple. "You're going to have fun on tour with Lyssa."

Grace wrapped her arms around him, pressing her forehead into his chest. "I'm going to miss you, though."

He held her, stroking her hair. "I'll come see you in Cleveland, and Boston. And maybe some of the other stops. Our album should be done soon, so I'll have some downtime."

Lyssa's giggle echoed off the walls, and Grace looked up to see Zeus chasing her down the alley between the storage units, spanking her butt lightly with the end of a guitar cord. "Giddyap, horsey!"

"Stop it, you cretin!"

The two came to a stop in front of Nelson and Grace, panting slightly. Lyssa reached out and took Zeus's hand.

"We got everything?"

Grace nodded. Nelson went to close the storage unit.

They all grabbed the last pieces of equipment and headed back for the van. Zeus and Lyssa walked in front, Lyssa laughing at Zeus's impression of a punk rock elephant.

Inez had finally decided that she'd rather be with Nicole, after all, which had been okay with Zeus, since he and Lyssa had been getting closer. Grace thought it was a much better match, and so far it hadn't affected their musical relationship. They were scheduled to start on their eight-country tour in five days, Grace in tow.

Inez had felt so bad that she'd been the one inadvertently passing info to Duke that she'd bought Zeus a new guitar and Grace a new laptop.

Nelson walked beside Grace, carrying her heavy amp. "You decided which agent you're going to sign with for your book?"

Grace chewed her cheek. Since she'd written an article about what had occurred with Marla and Duke, several agents had approached her about writing a full-length book with all the details of their kidnapping, and an expose on Marla and Duke's sordid web of lies and deceit. It was an epic tale; the police investigation for the upcoming trial, and Grace's own investigation, had uncovered a ruthless manipulation of facts for profit. Duke had scripted his clients' lives in order to increase their notoriety, and Marla had helped by reporting Duke's version of the truth. Duke had made money off his clients' sales, and Marla off writing about it.

Both of them were facing forty-five-year sentences for kidnapping, attempted murder, and racketeering. Prosecutors were confident they'd get convictions on all counts.

This story, and Grace's part in it, was something the public was clamoring to hear. Five publishers had offered her deals with seven figure advances, and agents were jostling to get in on the deal. Not only that, but *High Note* had contracted with her for a series of three exclusive articles about touring with Lyssa Medlin and had offered her way more money than she'd been expecting.

"I don't know," Grace finally said. "I might not need an agent, to tell you the truth."

Nelson grinned. "Yeah, I had a bad experience with my last one."

Grace snorted.

THE END

www.ingramcontent.com/pod-product-compliance
Lightning Source LLC
Chambersburg PA
CBHW061615190726
48288CB00007B/2326